8/21

~~THE A~~ ~~D OF~~

~~THE WORLD'S GREATEST SUPERHERO~~

SUPER DWEEB AND THE PENCIL OF DESTINY

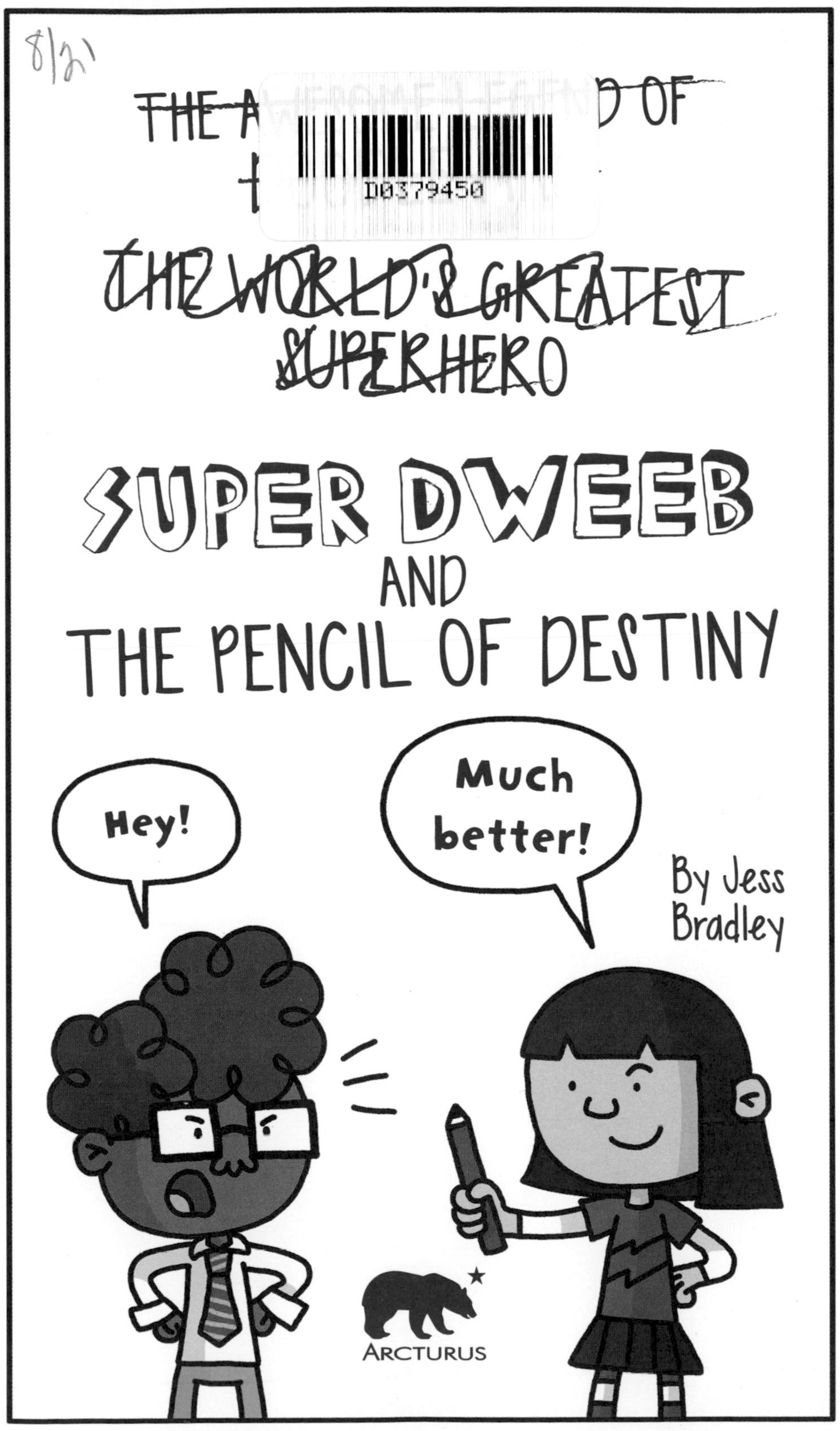
Hey!
Much better!

By Jess Bradley

ARCTURUS

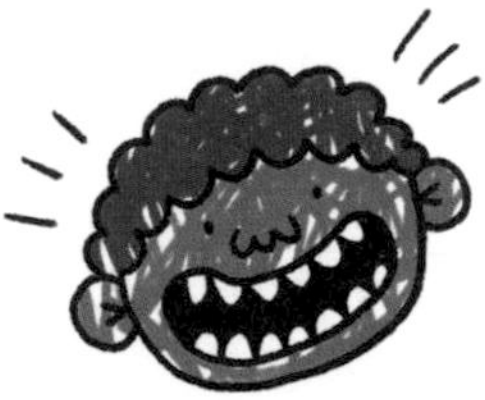

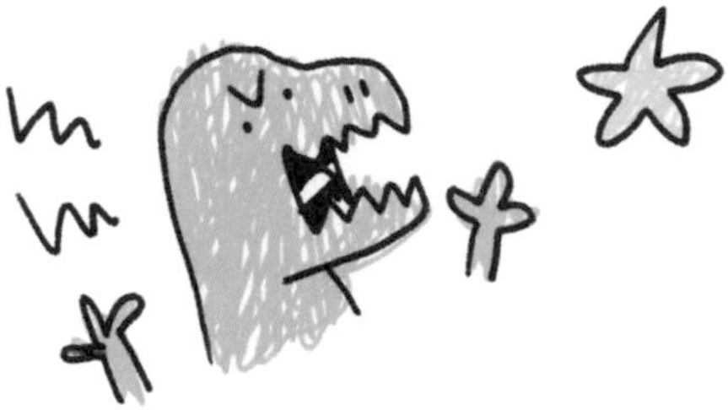

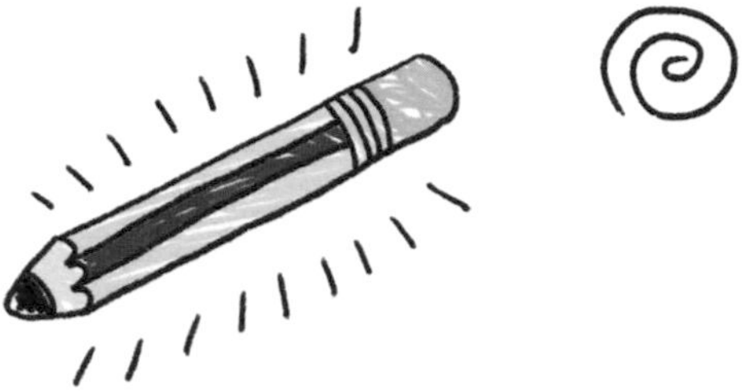

ARCTURUS

This edition published in 2021 by Arcturus Publishing Limited, 26/27 Bickels Yard, 151–153 Bermondsey Street, London SE1 3HA

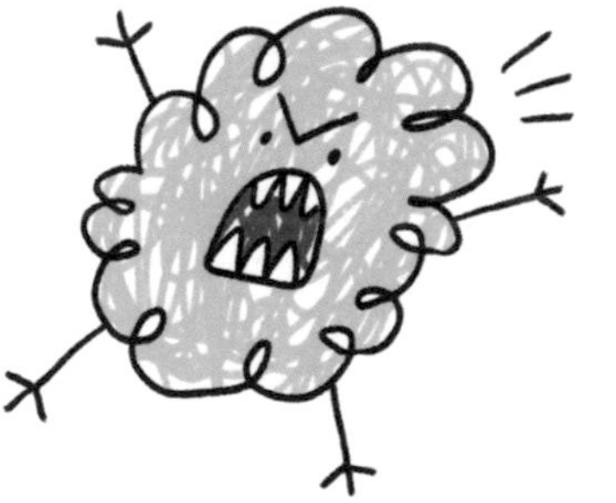

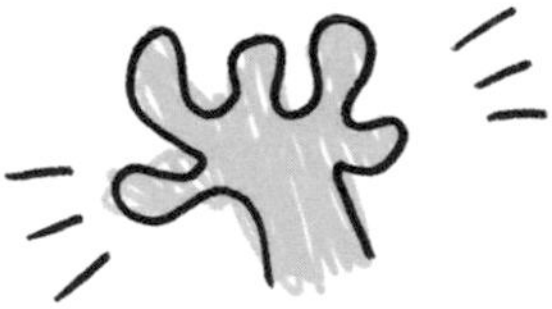

Words and pictures: Jess Bradley
Design: Stefan Holliland
Original concept: Joe Harris
Art direction: Rosie Bellwood

ISBN: 978-1-3988-0245-2
CH007132NT
Supplier 13, Date 0521, Print run 10766

Printed in China

Hi, I'm ANDY. Nice to meet you, person reading this! I'll call you P.R.T. for short. (You're cool with that, right, P.R.T.?) I'm a pretty normal kid. A bit dweeby, maybe. I can't catch a **football** or dance but I can draw pretty much ANYUTHING. Except for hands, which are really hard. This is the incredible TRUE STORY of how I became a

SUPERHERO.

(Yes, really!)

LOOK!
IT'S ME!

DOODLING

Andy?
Andy!

⭐ CONTENTS ⭐

Chapter 1 The Trouble with Mr. Squibb

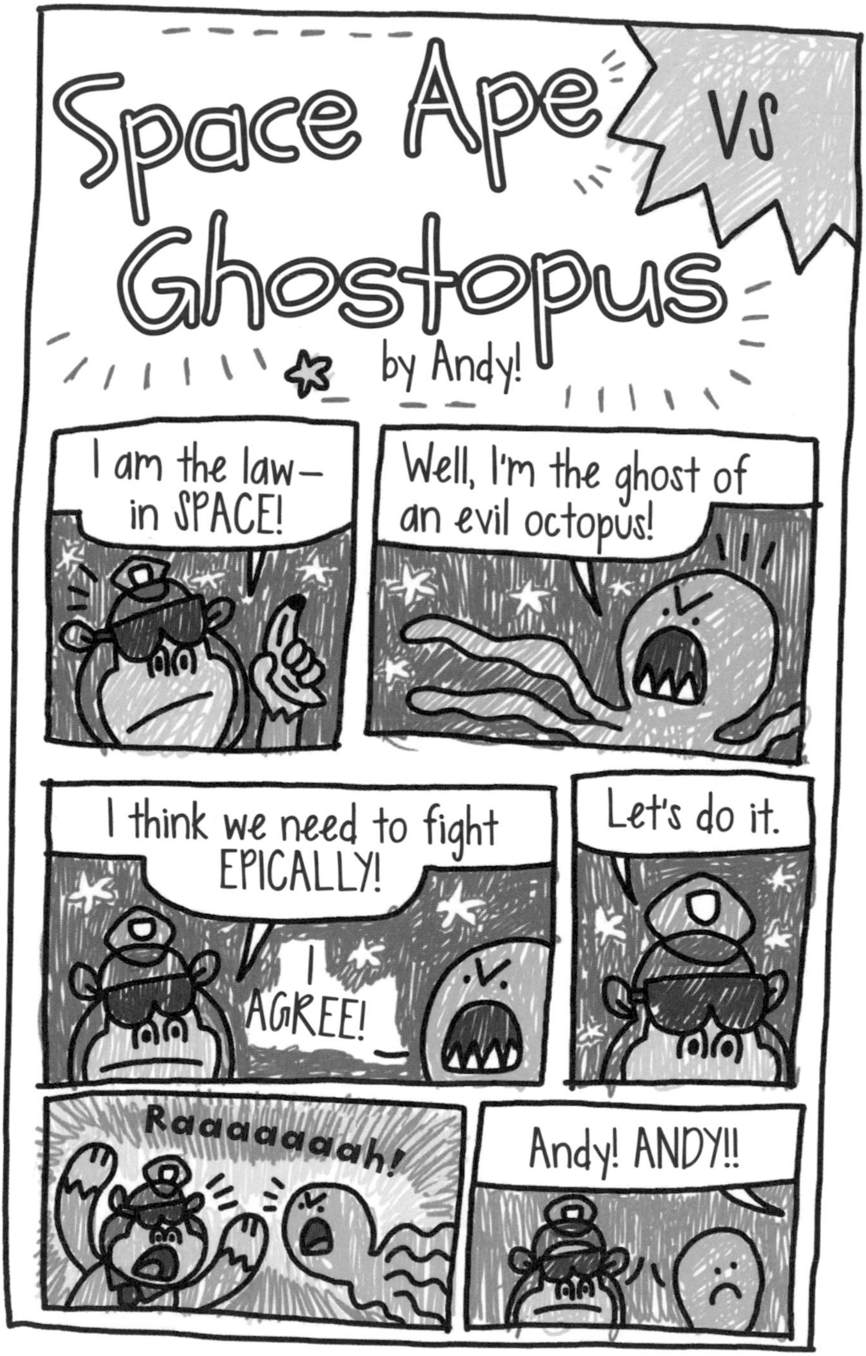
Space Ape VS Ghostopus
by Andy!
I am the law—in SPACE!
Well, I'm the ghost of an evil octopus!
I think we need to fight EPICALLY!
I AGREE!
Let's do it.
Raaaaaaaah!
Andy! ANDY!!

"Andy! ANDY! ANNNDDDYYY! Are you paying attention in class or are you DRAWING AGAIN?"

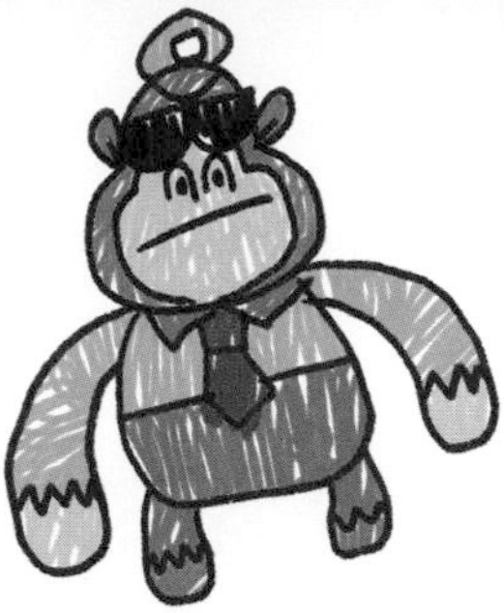

Uh-oh. This sounded like a problem that not even **ACE SILVERBACK**, maverick space-gorilla cop, could solve. I had been completely lost in thought, happily doodling the latest cosmic adventure in my awesome **SPACE APE**™ series.

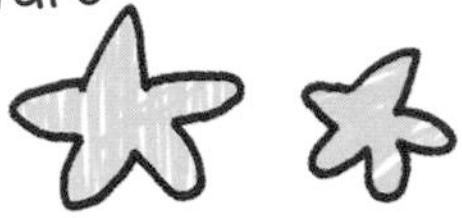

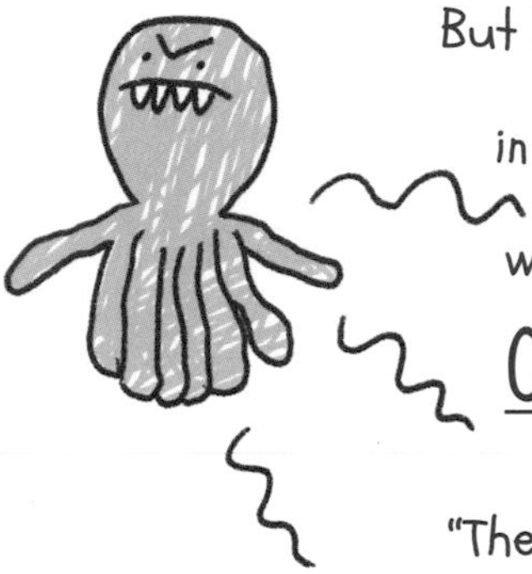

But I wasn't being threatened by evil alien octopods in the ghastly gamma quadrant. No, the truth was much worse—I was in Mr. Squibb's MATH CLASS. And Mr. Squibb did NOT look happy.

"The last time I checked, we were not studying ART. We were studying algebra. And these ... monkeys and squid ... are definitely **NOT ALGEBRA!**"

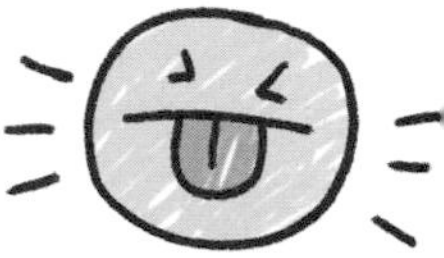

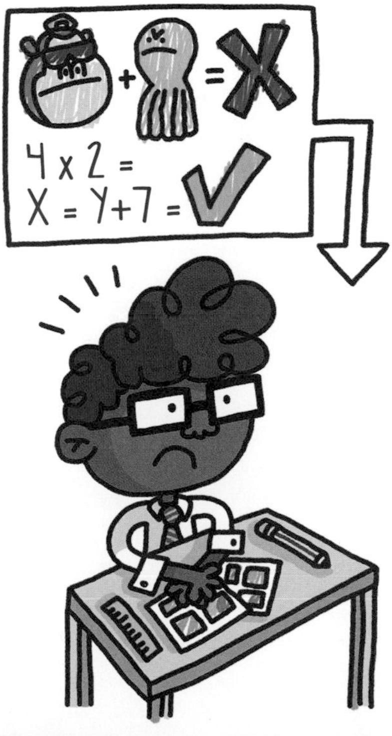

4 x 2 =
X = Y+7 =

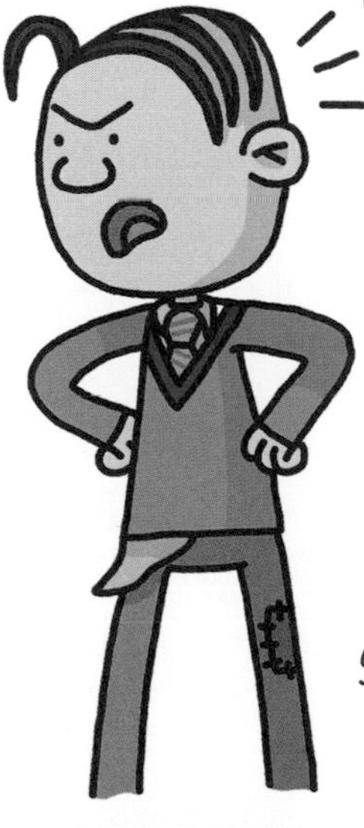

"Um, it's an ape and an octopus actually," I mumbled. "Not a squibb—I mean, a squid." Several of the class sniggered.

"I don't **CARE!**" said Mr. Squibb, "Drawing pictures won't get you anywhere in life."

Mr. Squibb is <u>SUPER-BORING</u>. If I had to write reports for my teachers, this is what I would send home to his parents.

MR. SQUIBB'S REPORT CARD
Your son, Mr. Squibb, has no imagination. Like, literally, zero. His favorite book is the dishwasher manual. He can suck the fun and excitement out of absolutely anything—like some kind of super-powerful fun vacuum cleaner. (Except that sounds sort of cool, so forget that.) Grade: ZZZ (for snoring).

"Are you paying attention, ANDY?" Somehow, Mr. Squibb was still speaking. "As I was saying—that's why today we will be taking a field trip. A highly educational field trip. Everyone take a leaflet and pass it on."

I took one of the leaflets and read it.

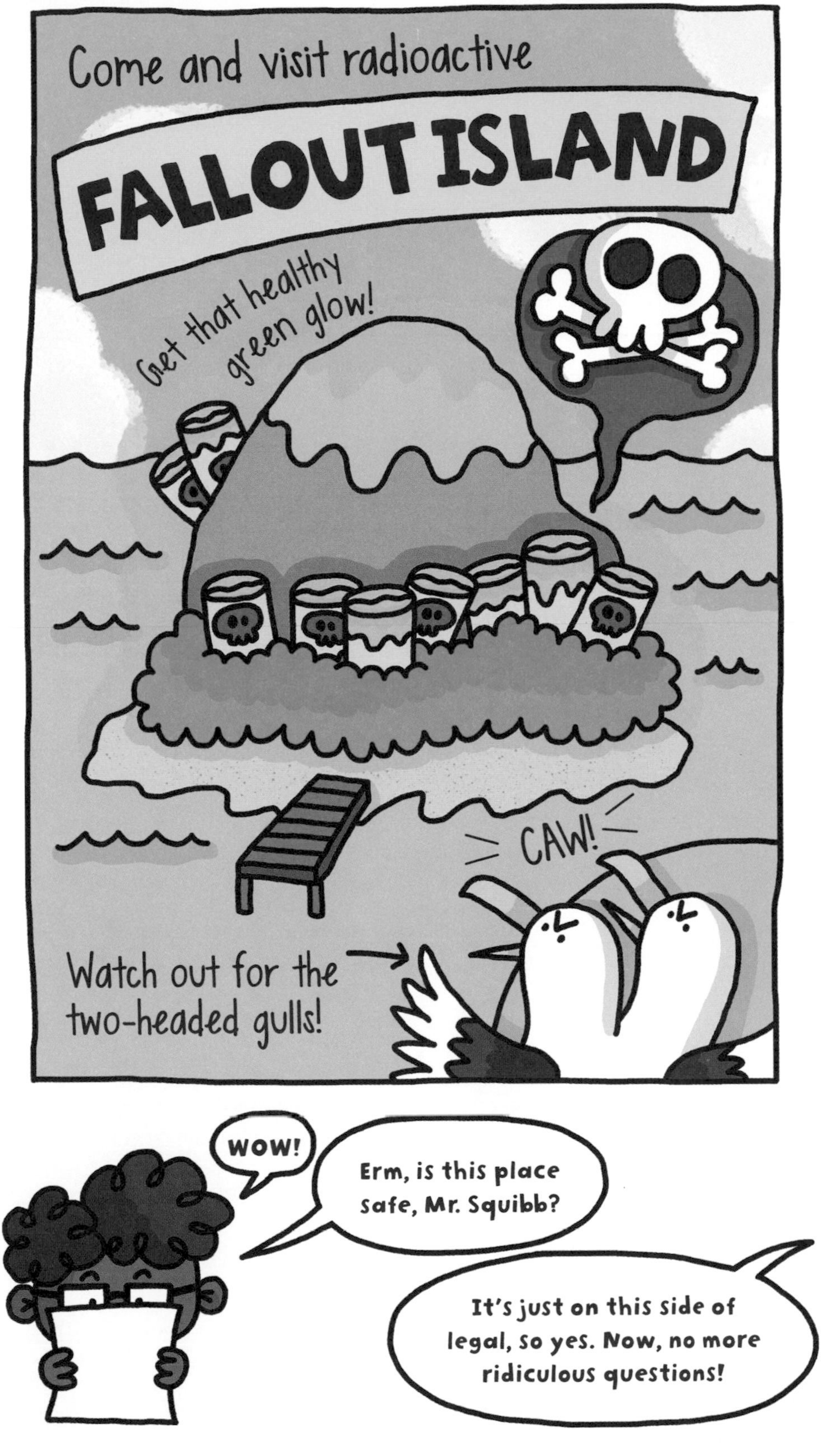
Come and visit radioactive
FALLOUT ISLAND
Get that healthy green glow!
CAW!
Watch out for the two-headed gulls!
WOW!
Erm, is this place safe, Mr. Squibb?
It's just on this side of legal, so yes. Now, no more ridiculous questions!

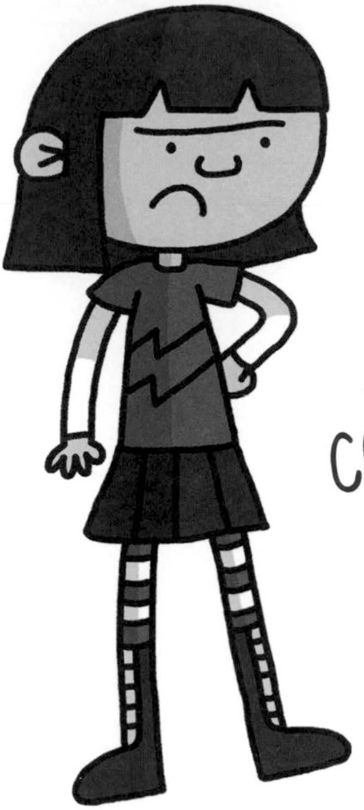

"We also have a new student! This is **MONA**. Why don't you tell us a little bit about yourself?"

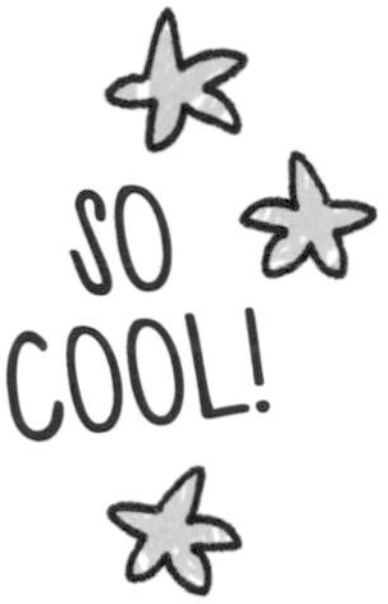
SO COOL!

"We moved here from Battsburg so my dad could study AI at the university. This town smells funny. <u>***NOT GOOD FUNNY***</u>."

"Um, super! Well, why don't you go and take a seat with Andy? In fact, you can be his **BUDDY** on the school trip!"

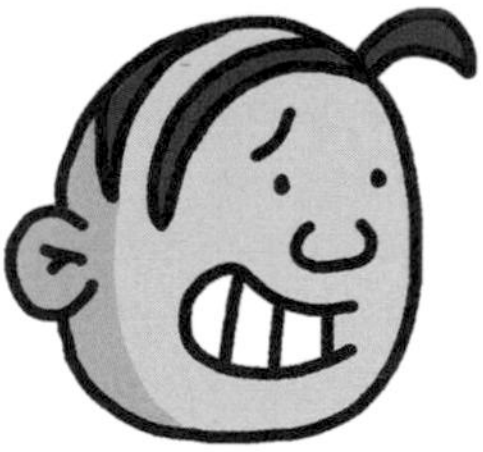

Of course everyone laughed. A **COOL** person being buddies with ***ME***?

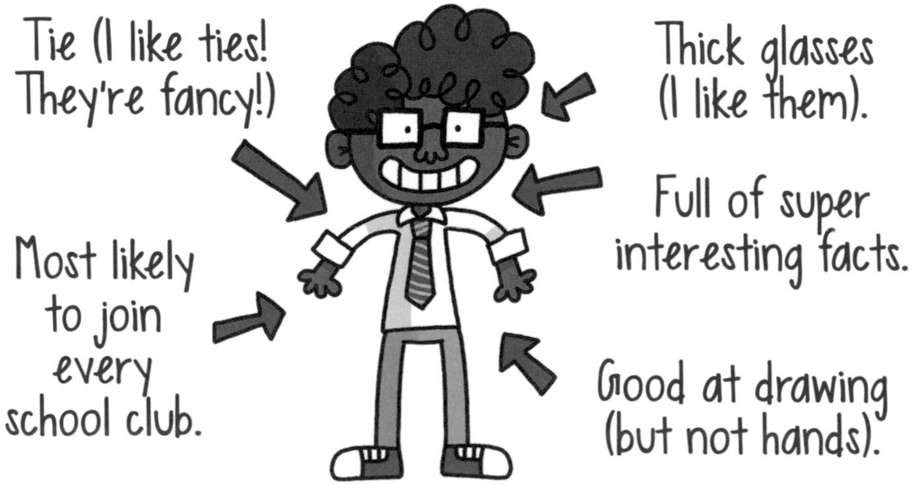
Tie (I like ties! They're fancy!)
Thick glasses (I like them).
Full of super interesting facts.
Most likely to join every school club.
Good at drawing (but not hands).

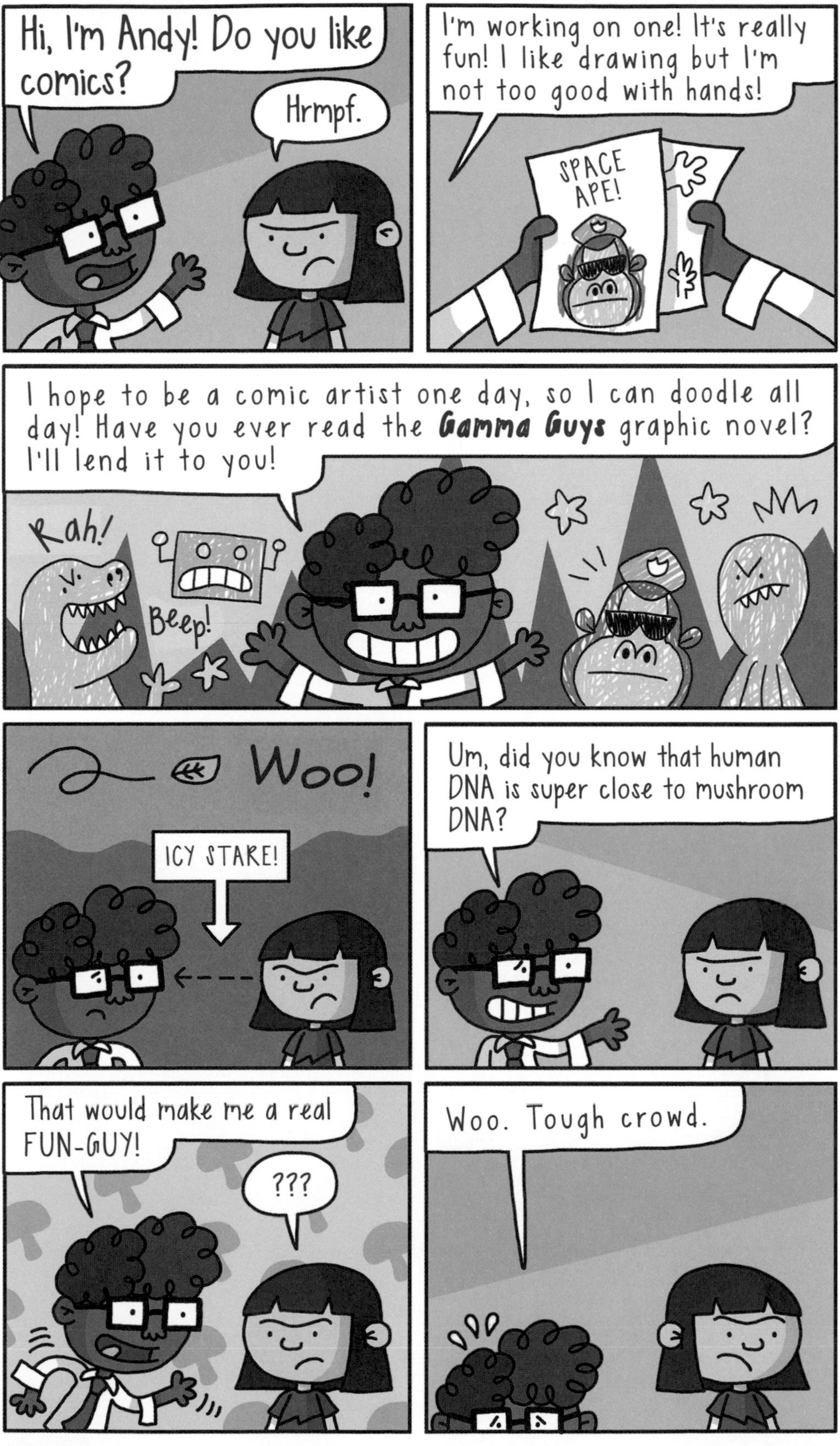
Hi, I'm Andy! Do you like comics?
Hrmpf.
I'm working on one! It's really fun! I like drawing but I'm not too good with hands!
SPACE APE!
I hope to be a comic artist one day, so I can doodle all day! Have you ever read the Gamma Guys graphic novel? I'll lend it to you!
Rah!
Beep!
Woo!
ICY STARE!
Um, did you know that human DNA is super close to mushroom DNA?
That would make me a real FUN-GUY!
???
Woo. Tough crowd.

"Hey, New Girl! Have fun being paired with UBER-DORK! Ha ha ha!"

GOOD ONE!

YEAH! DORK!

HA HA! HEE!

Ugh, it's Mean Mike! Every class has that one kid destined to be a super villain and Mike is in MINE! We've been in the same class since first grade and he lives to make my life a MISERY! (I think he's just jealous of my drawing skills.)

Mike is always surrounded by his goons:

Goon 1

CASSIE:
Laughs like a
hyena in pain.

Goon 2

PETE:
Big and not
too bright.

Goon 3

TYLER:
Eats nothing but
string cheese.

ME AND MEAN MIKE: A BRIEF HISTORY

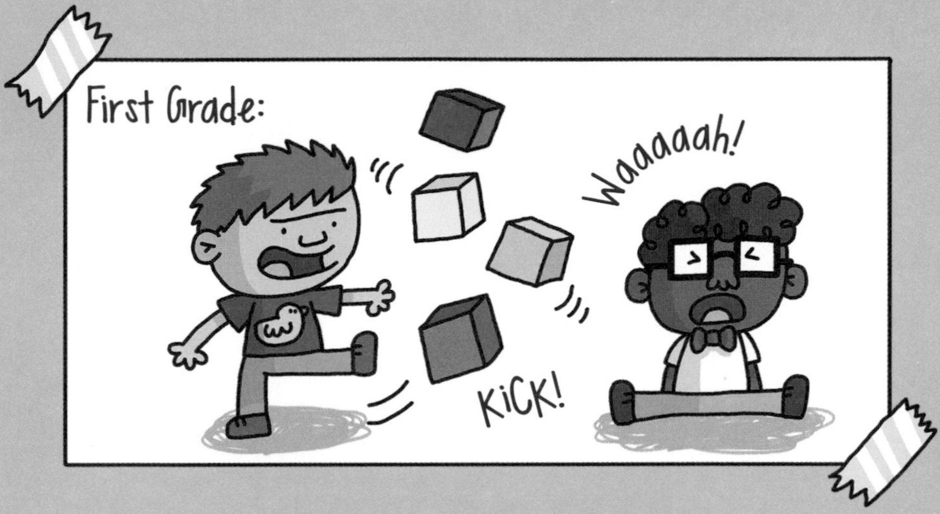
First Grade:
Waaaaah!
KICK!

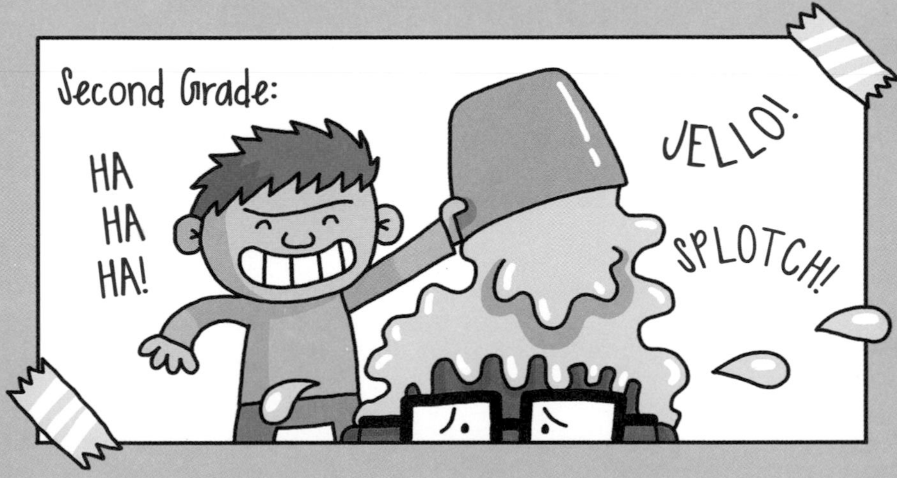
Second Grade:
HA
HA
HA!
JELLO!
SPLOTCH!

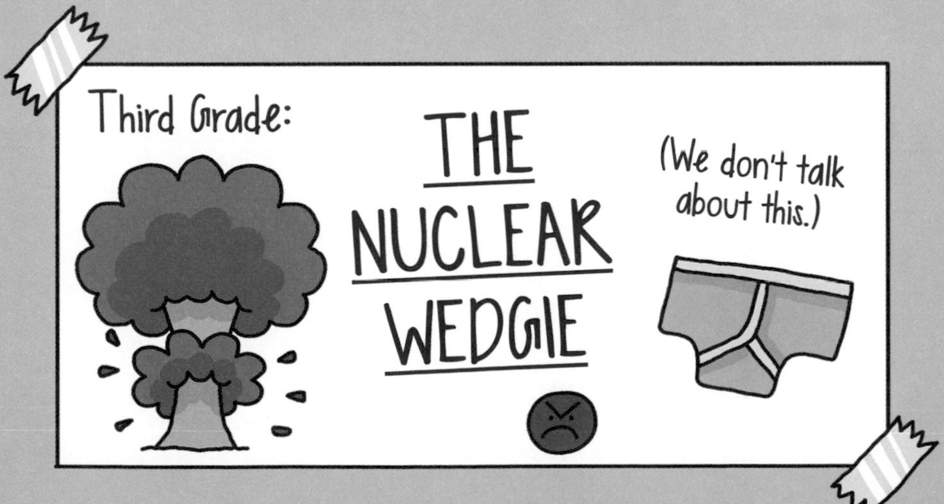
Third Grade:
THE
NUCLEAR
WEDGIE
(We don't talk
about this.)

Chapter 2 **The World's Worst Field Trip**

Soon ...

"Okay everyone, on the bus!" said Mr. Squibb.

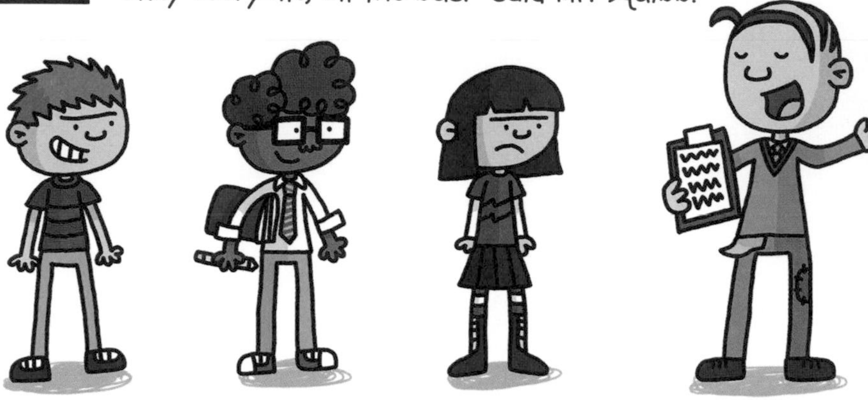

I couldn't wait to get to Fallout Island and do some sketching.

Maybe I'd get some cool ideas for my Space Ape comic!

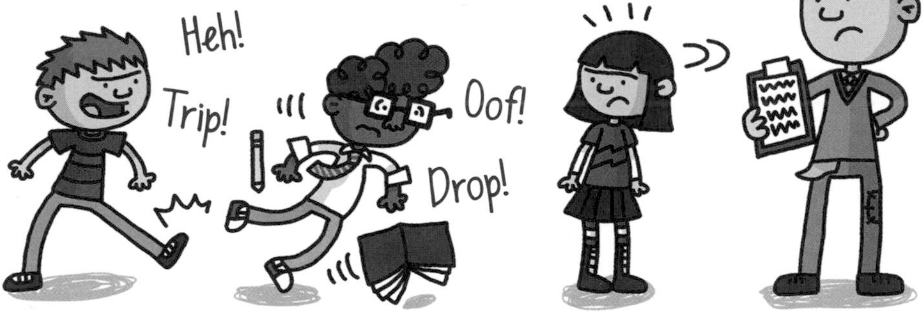
Heh!
Trip!
Oof!
Drop!

"Now, Mike, you've already got three detentions this week

and it's only 10a.m. on Monday!" said Mr. Squibb.

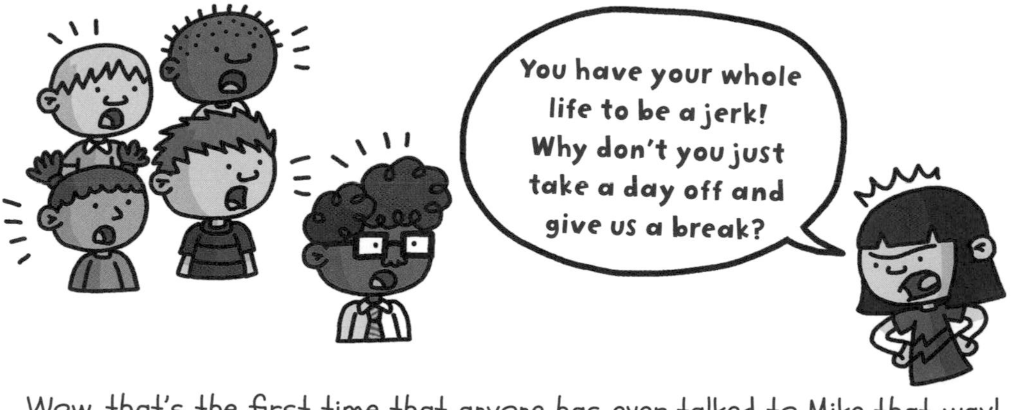
You have your whole life to be a jerk! Why don't you just take a day off and give us a break?

Wow, that's the first time that anyone has ever talked to Mike that way!

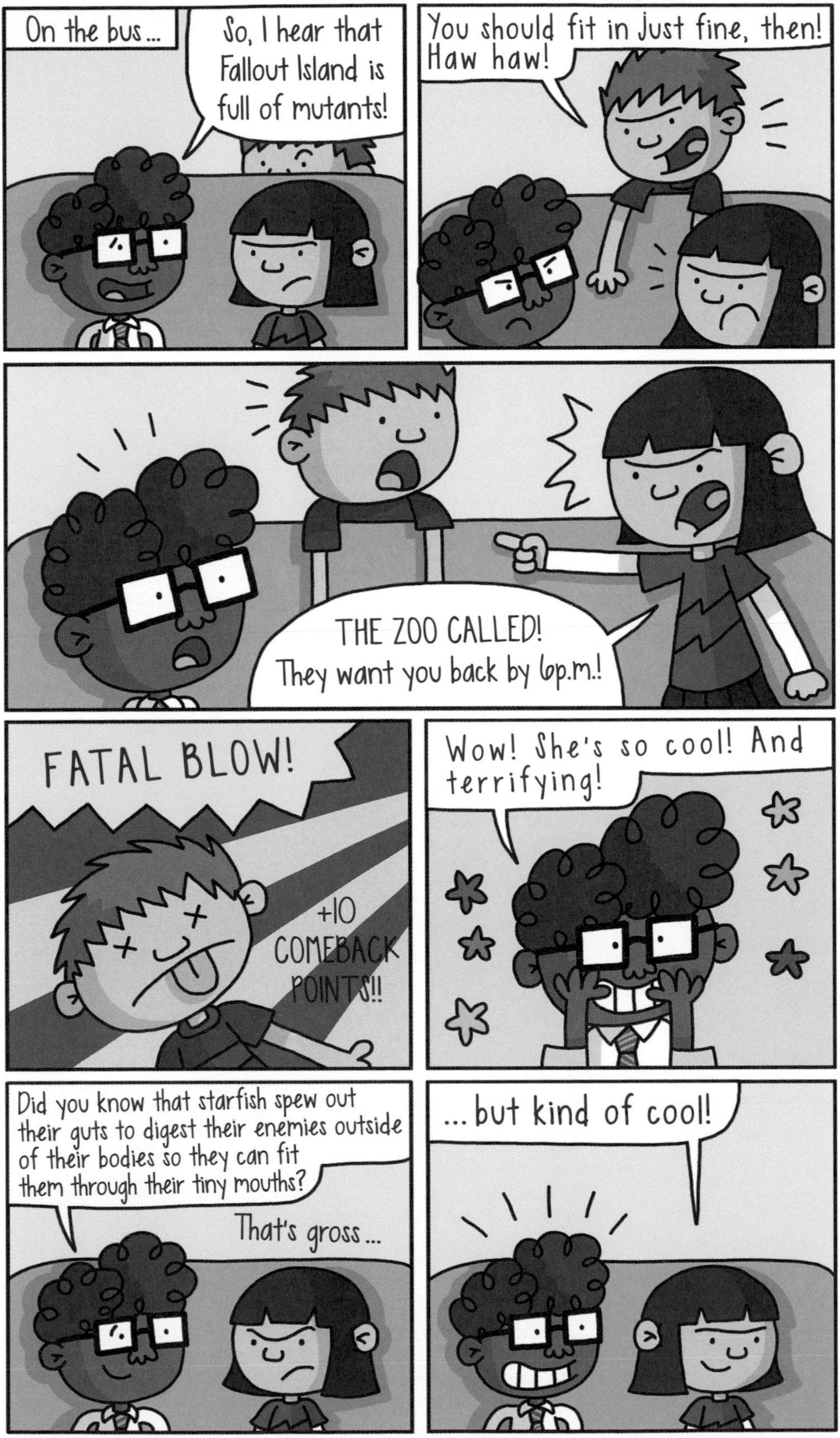
On the bus ...
So, I hear that Fallout Island is full of mutants!
You should fit in just fine, then! Haw haw!
THE ZOO CALLED! They want you back by 6p.m.!
FATAL BLOW!
+10 COMEBACK POINTS!!
Wow! She's so cool! And terrifying!
Did you know that starfish spew out their guts to digest their enemies outside of their bodies so they can fit them through their tiny mouths?
That's gross ...
... but kind of cool!

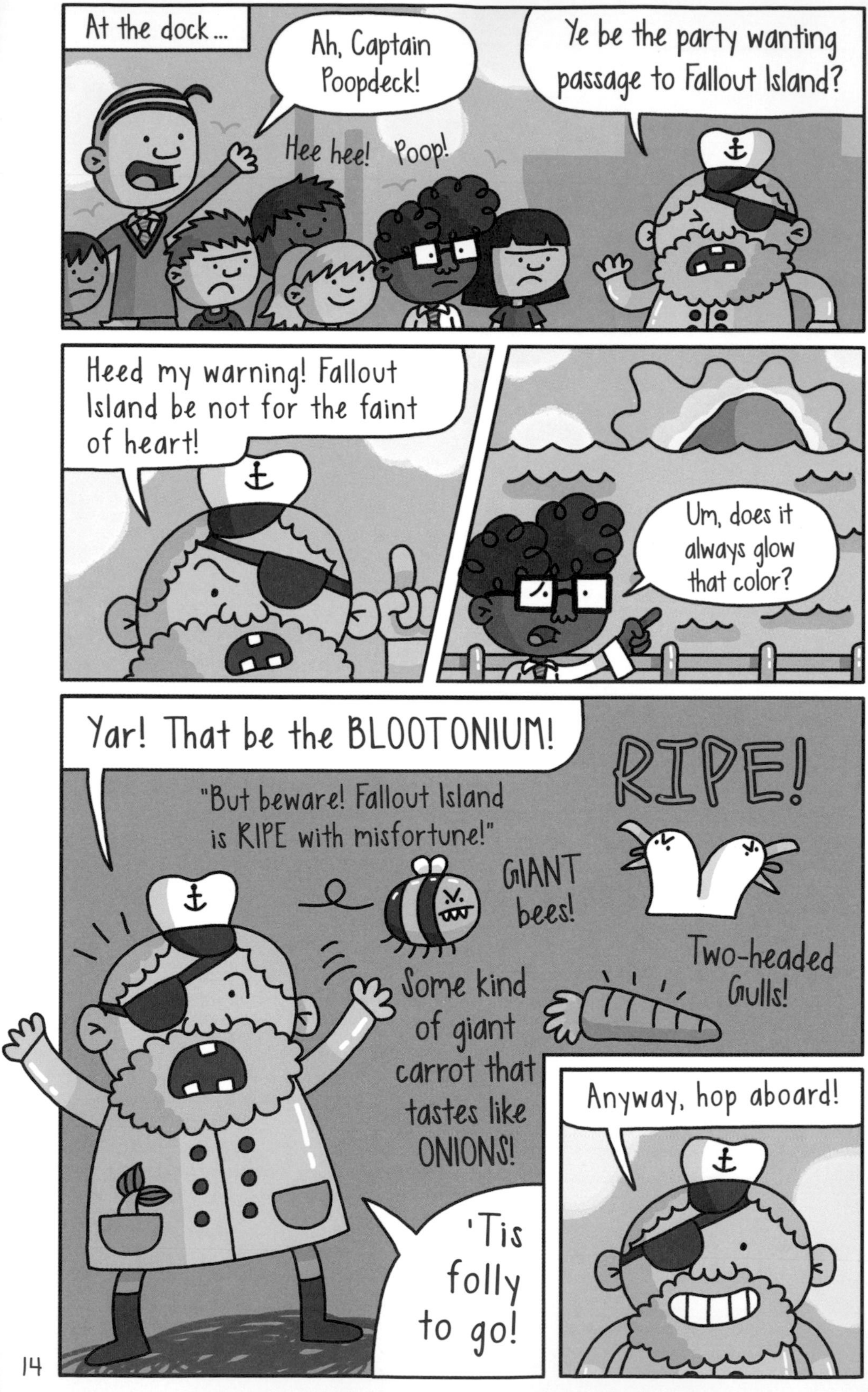
At the dock...
Ah, Captain Poopdeck!
Hee hee!
Poop!
Ye be the party wanting passage to Fallout Island?
Heed my warning! Fallout Island be not for the faint of heart!
Um, does it always glow that color?
Yar! That be the BLOOTONIUM!
"But beware! Fallout Island is RIPE with misfortune!"
RIPE!
GIANT bees!
Two-headed Gulls!
Some kind of giant carrot that tastes like ONIONS!
'Tis folly to go!
Anyway, hop aboard!

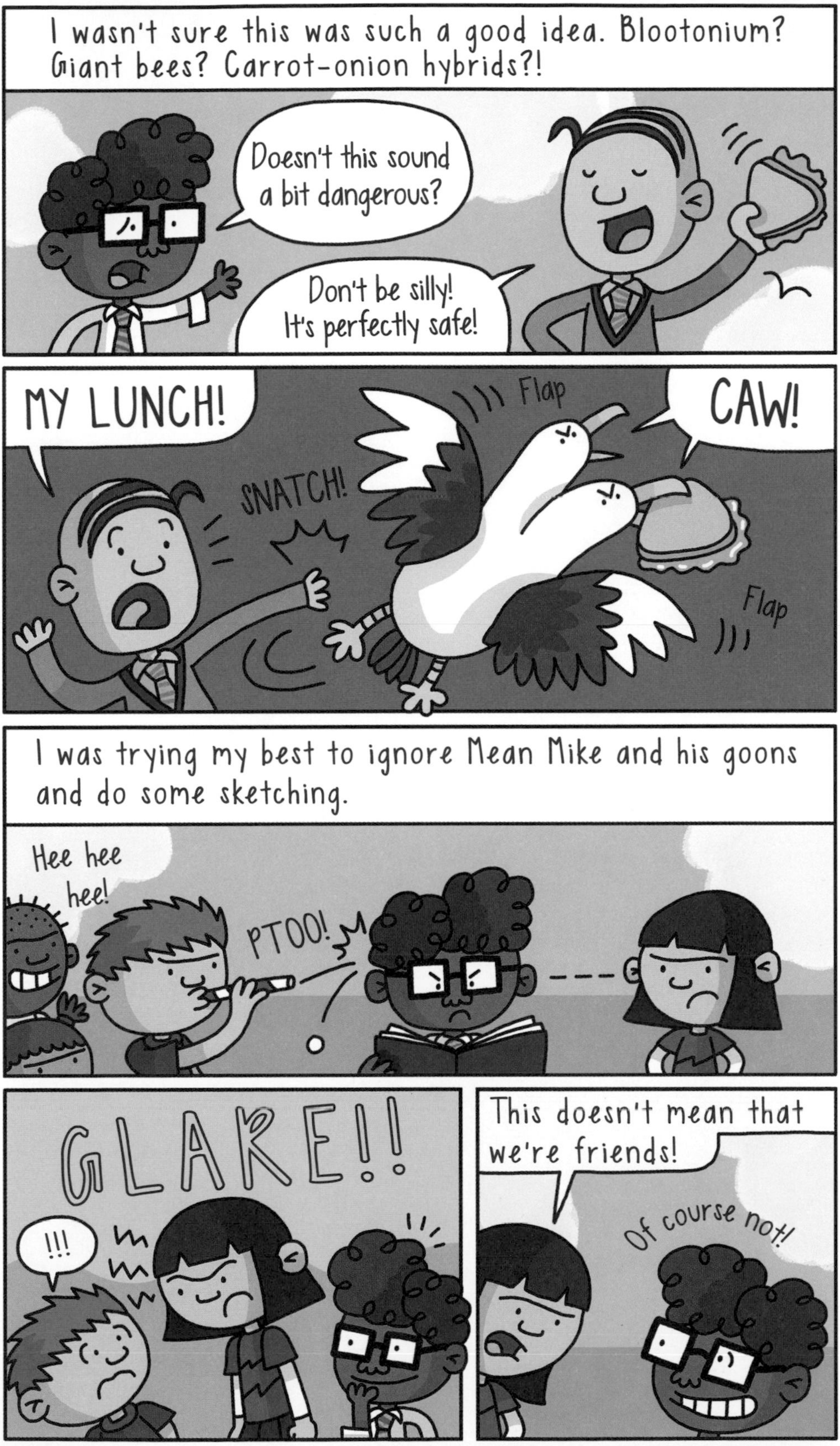
I wasn't sure this was such a good idea. Blootonium? Giant bees? Carrot-onion hybrids?!
Doesn't this sound a bit dangerous?
Don't be silly! It's perfectly safe!
MY LUNCH!
SNATCH!
Flap
CAW!
Flap
I was trying my best to ignore Mean Mike and his goons and do some sketching.
Hee hee hee!
PTOO!
GLARE!!
!!!
This doesn't mean that we're friends!
Of course not!

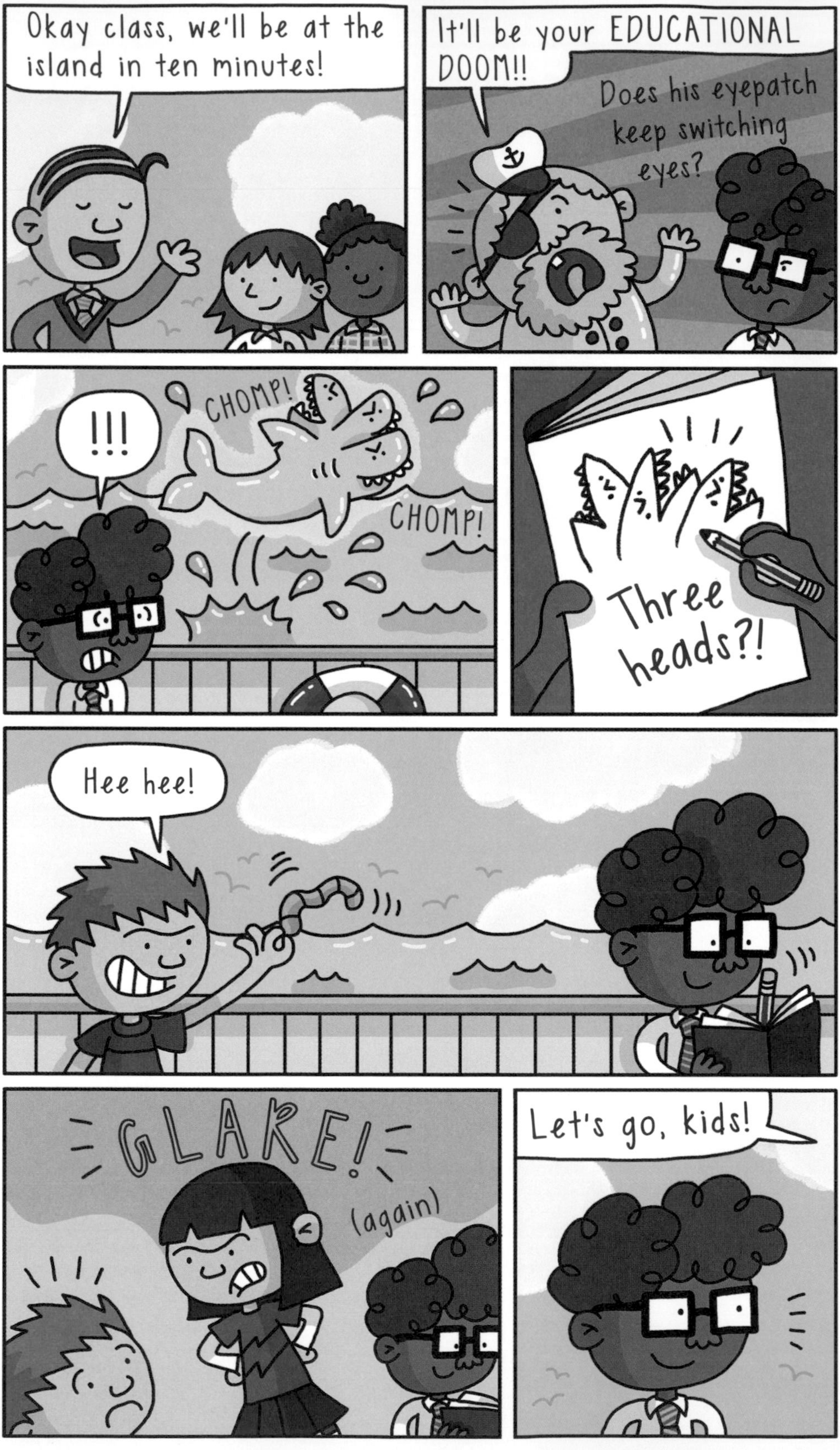
Okay class, we'll be at the island in ten minutes!
It'll be your EDUCATIONAL DOOM!!
Does his eyepatch keep switching eyes?
!!!
CHOMP!
CHOMP!
Three heads?!
Hee hee!
GLARE!
(again)
Let's go, kids!

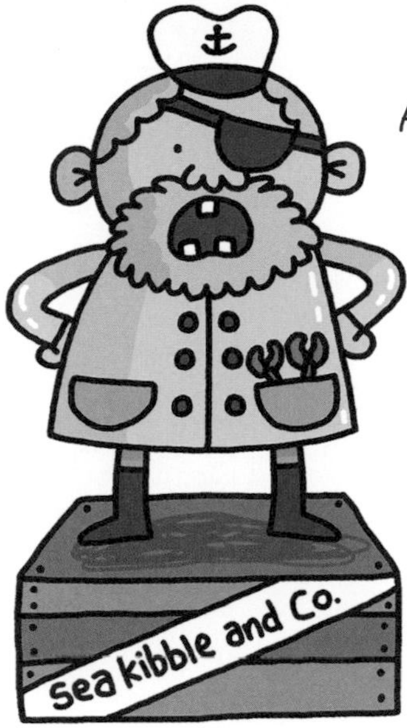
Sea kibble and Co.

And we were on FALLOUT ISLAND!

"Watch your step, children! Yar!" said Captain Poopdeck.

"Captain, why does your EYEPATCH keep switching eyes?" I asked.

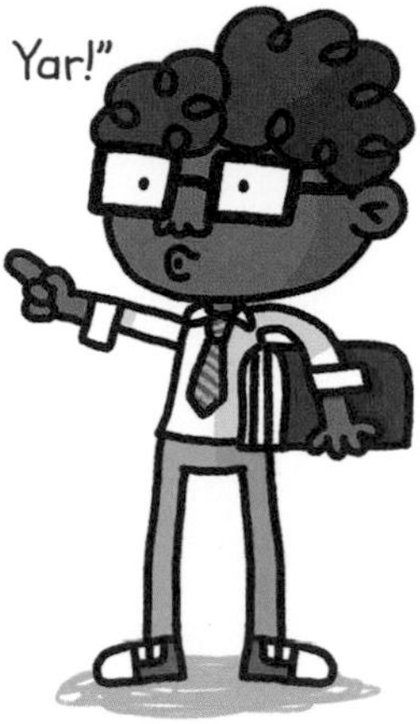

"I have no idea what ye be talking about! Yar!" said Captain Poopdeck.

Mr. Squibb rounded us all up and we headed off. For a radiation-filled HAZARD, it was actually pretty scenic!

"Okay class, time for a hike! Pay particular attention to the MUTATED flora!"

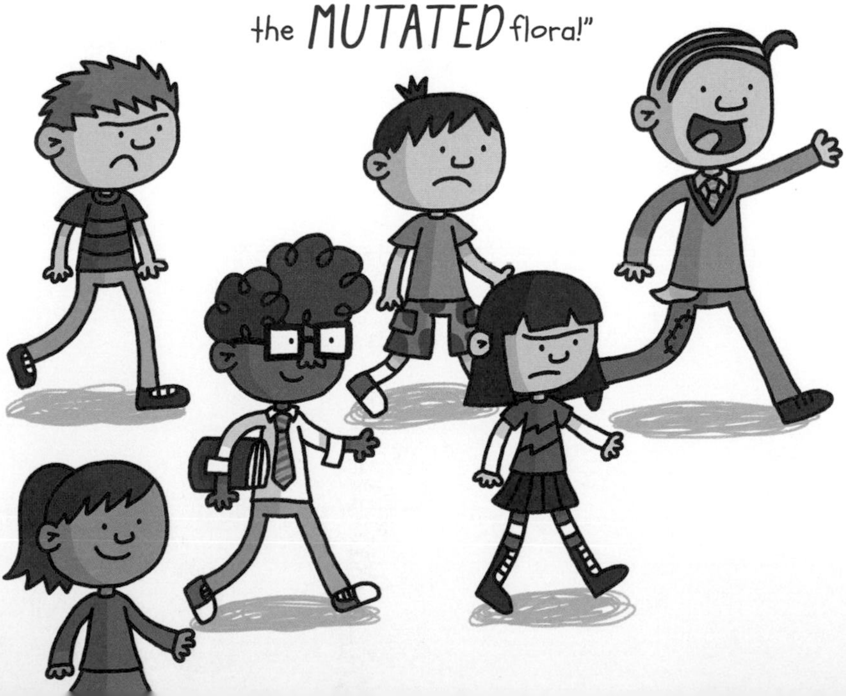

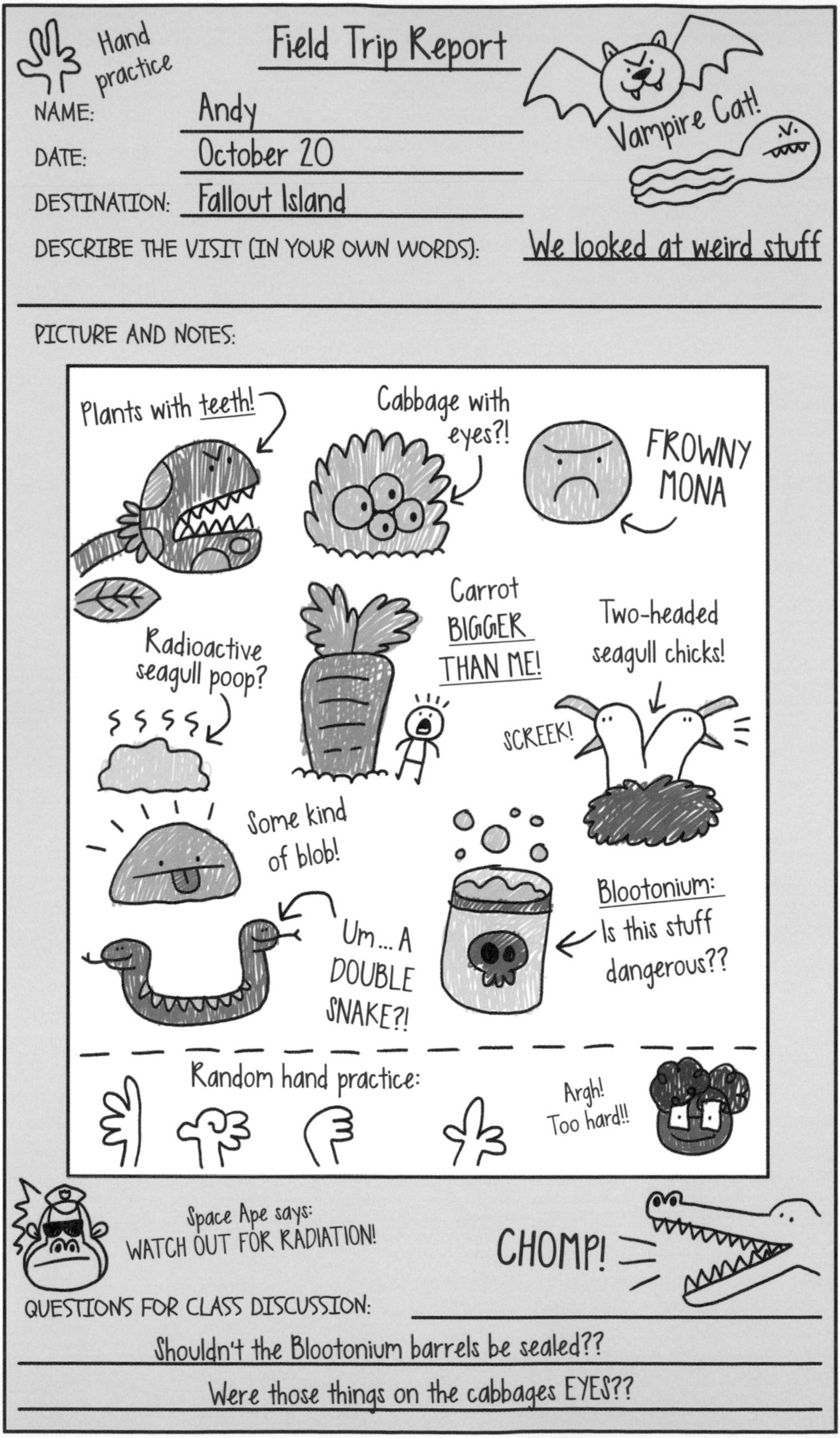

Hand practice
Field Trip Report
NAME: Andy
DATE: October 20
DESTINATION: Fallout Island
DESCRIBE THE VISIT (IN YOUR OWN WORDS): We looked at weird stuff
Vampire Cat!
PICTURE AND NOTES:
Plants with teeth!
Cabbage with eyes?!
FROWNY MONA
Radioactive seagull poop?
Carrot BIGGER THAN ME!
Two-headed seagull chicks!
SCREEK!
Some kind of blob!
Um... A DOUBLE SNAKE?!
Blootonium: Is this stuff dangerous??
Random hand practice:
Argh! Too hard!!
Space Ape says: WATCH OUT FOR RADIATION!
CHOMP!
QUESTIONS FOR CLASS DISCUSSION:
Shouldn't the Blootonium barrels be sealed??
Were those things on the cabbages EYES??

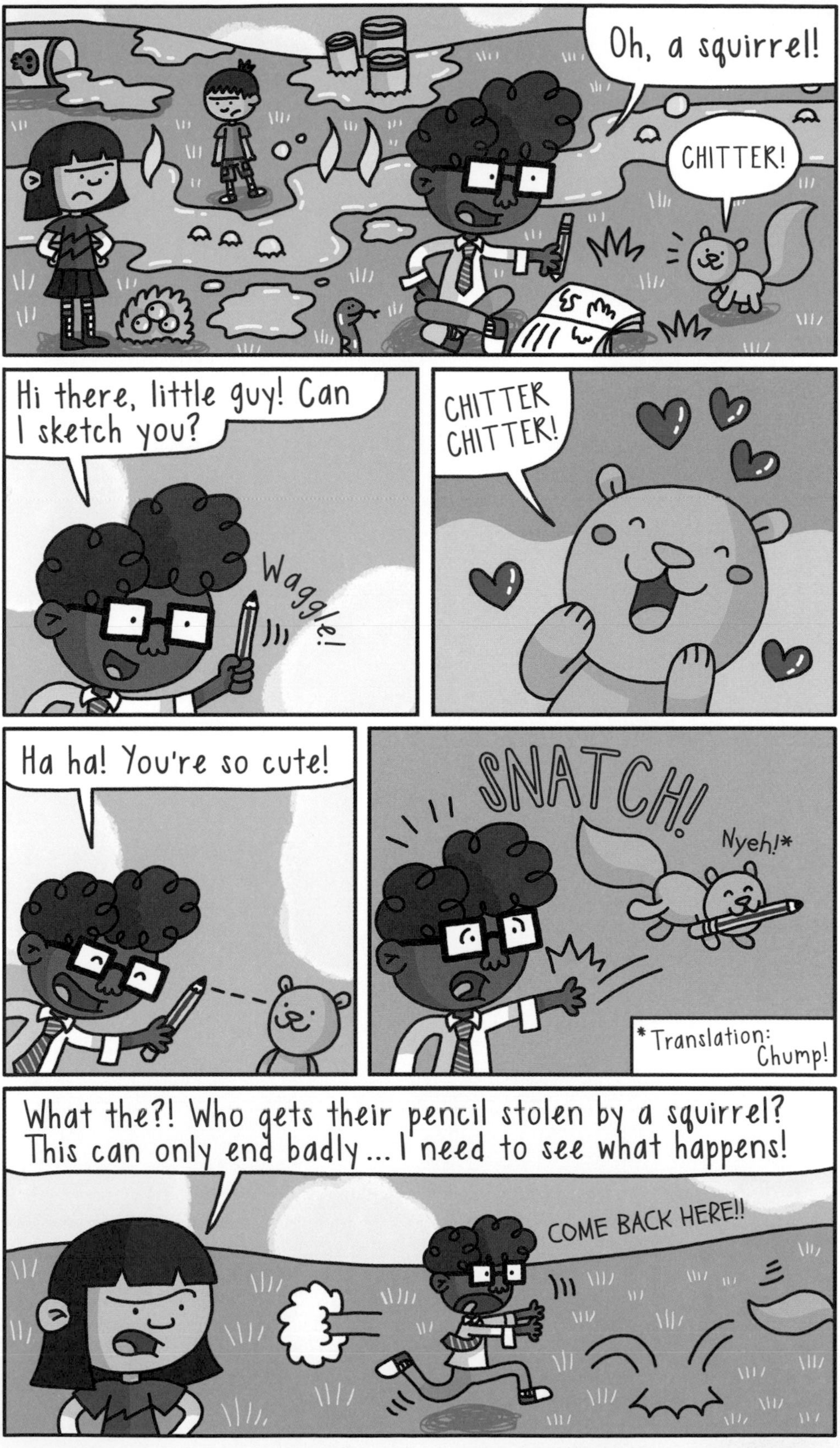
Oh, a squirrel!
CHITTER!
Hi there, little guy! Can I sketch you?
Waggle!
CHITTER CHITTER!
Ha ha! You're so cute!
SNATCH!
Nyeh!*
*Translation: Chump!
What the?! Who gets their pencil stolen by a squirrel? This can only end badly ... I need to see what happens!
COME BACK HERE!!

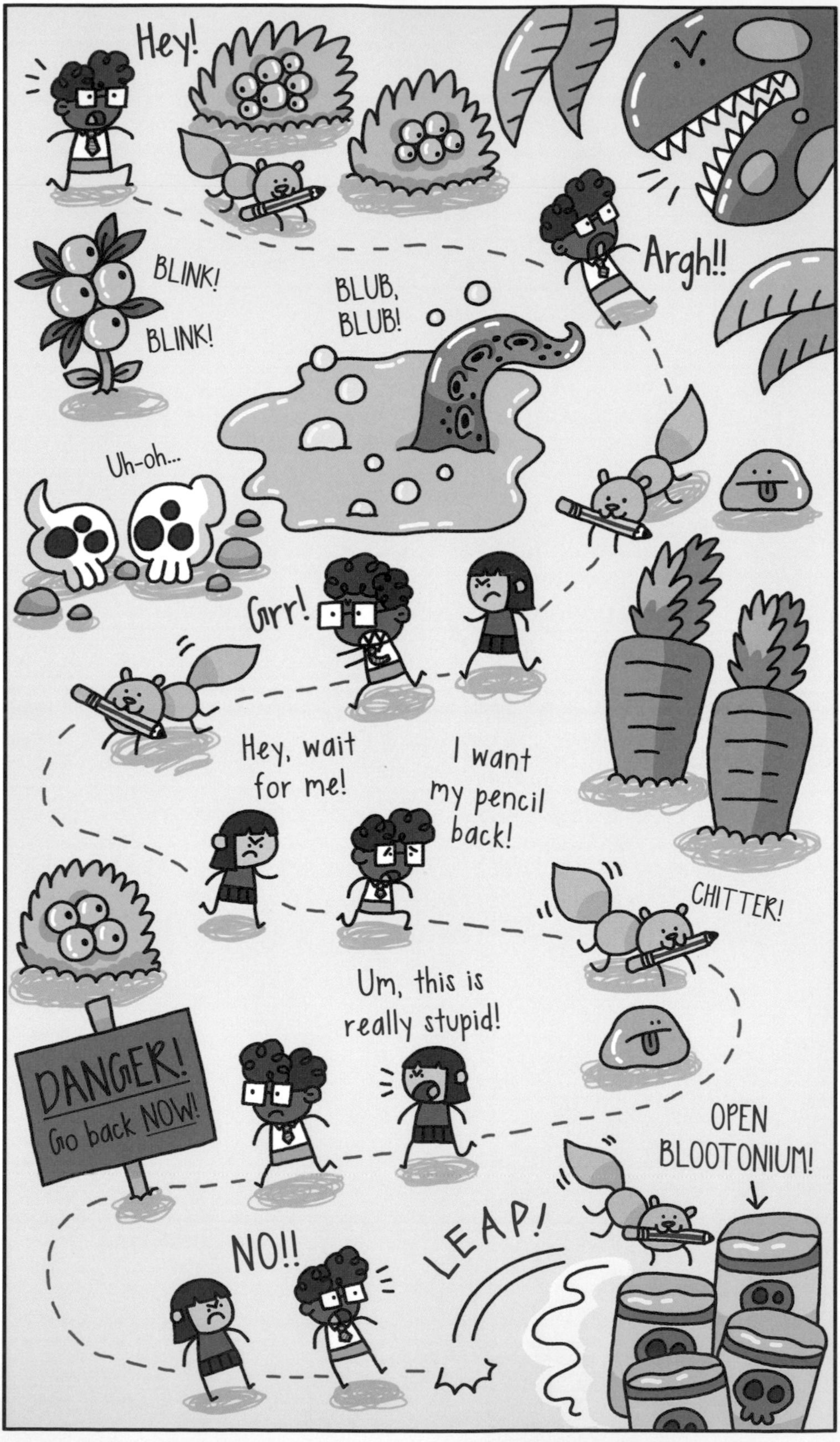
Hey!
Argh!!
BLINK!
BLINK!
BLUB, BLUB!
Uh-oh...
Grr!
Hey, wait for me!
I want my pencil back!
CHITTER!
Um, this is really stupid!
DANGER! Go back NOW!
OPEN BLOOTONIUM!
NO!!
LEAP!

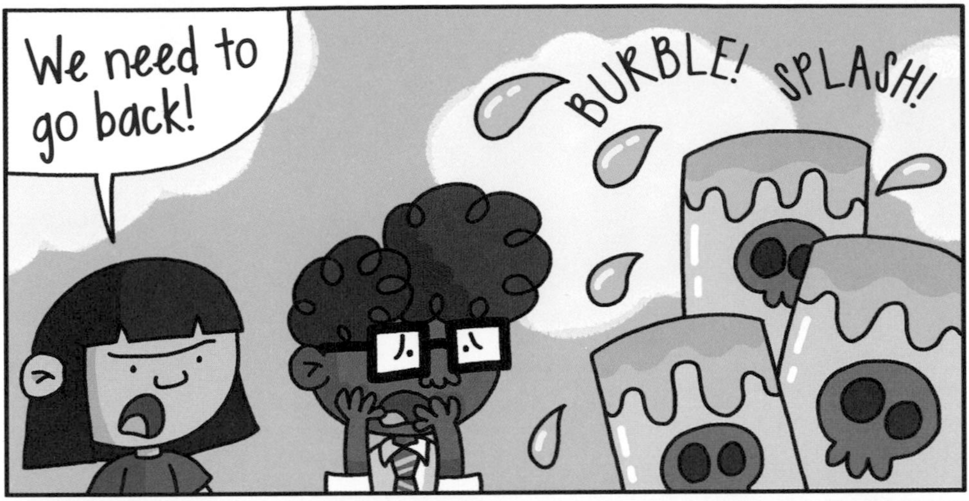
We need to go back!
BURBLE! SPLASH!

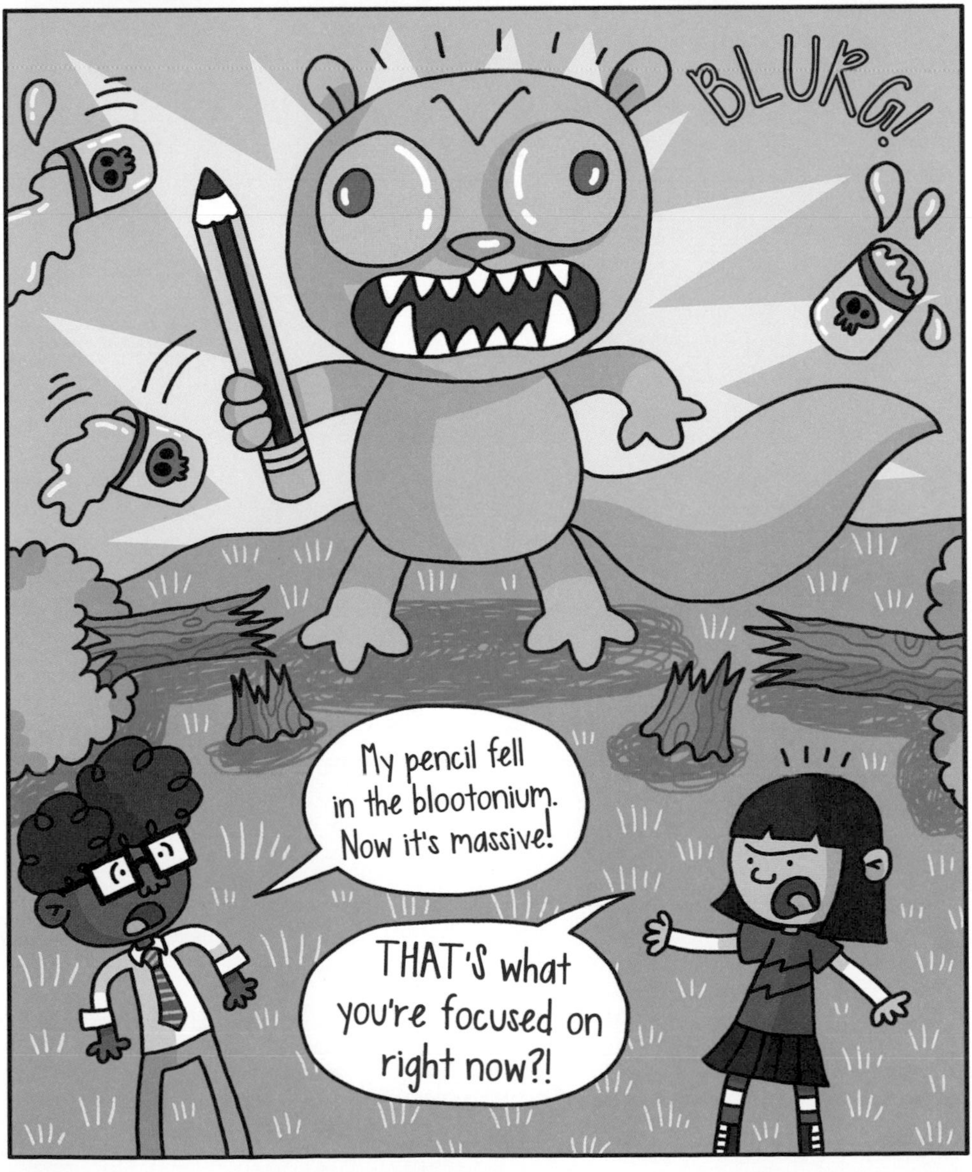
BLURG!
My pencil fell in the blootonium. Now it's massive!
THAT'S what you're focused on right now?!

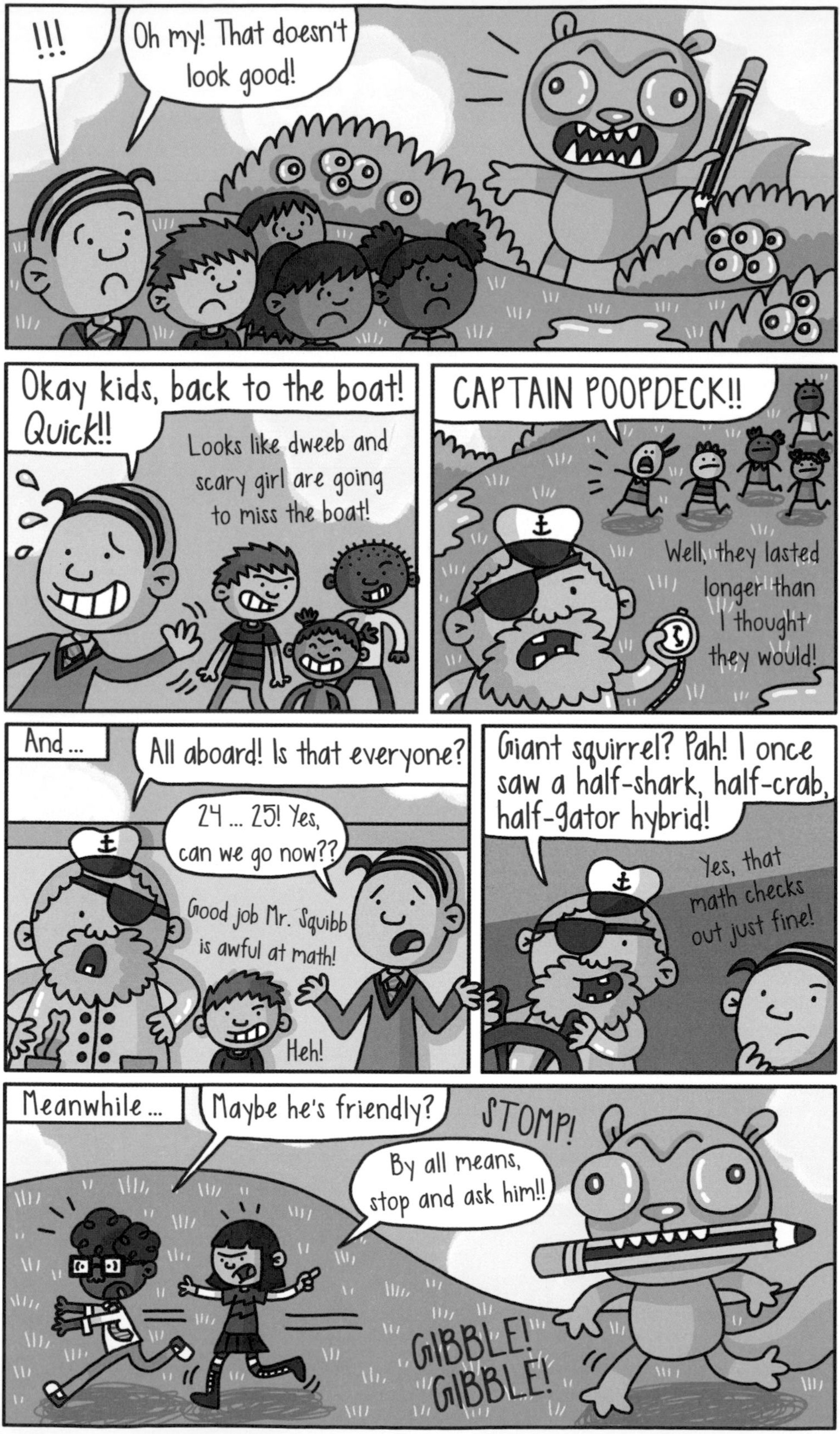
!!!
Oh my! That doesn't look good!
Okay kids, back to the boat! Quick!!
Looks like dweeb and scary girl are going to miss the boat!
CAPTAIN POOPDECK!!
Well, they lasted longer than I thought they would!
And ...
All aboard! Is that everyone?
24 ... 25! Yes, can we go now??
Good job Mr. Squibb is awful at math!
Heh!
Giant squirrel? Pah! I once saw a half-shark, half-crab, half-gator hybrid!
Yes, that math checks out just fine!
Meanwhile ...
Maybe he's friendly?
STOMP!
By all means, stop and ask him!!
GIBBLE! GIBBLE!

If Squirrelzilla hadn't been chasing us, I would have stopped to **SKETCH** him! We ran through the woods back to the dock.

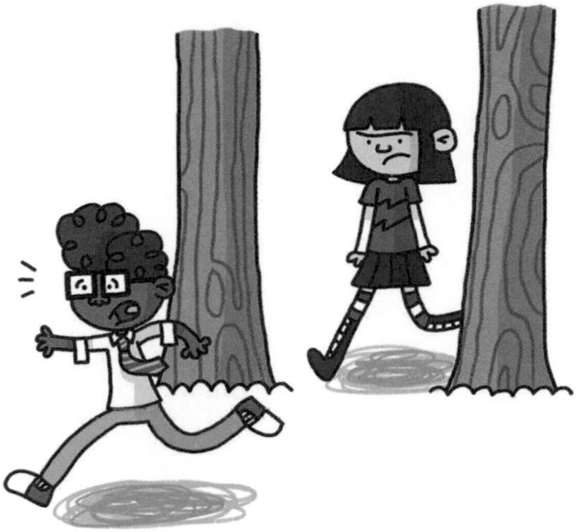

"Quick, through here! Maybe we can lose him!" I shouted.

Luckily, it looked like squirrelzillas weren't too **INTELLIGENT!**

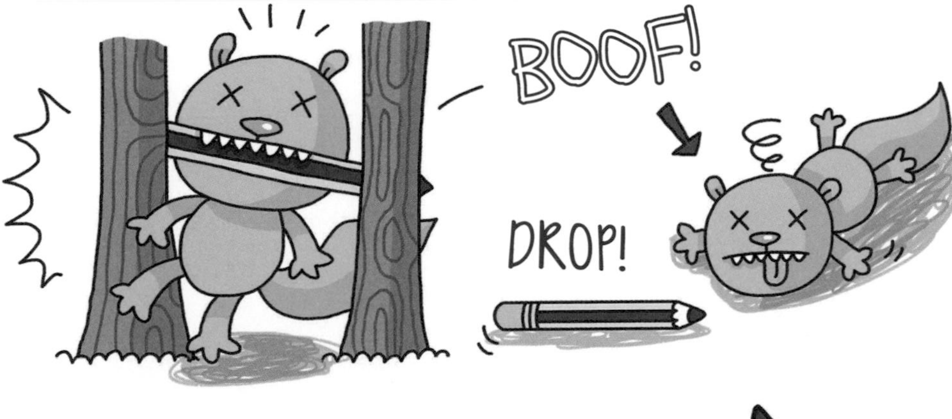
BOOF!
DROP!

I ran to grab my pencil.

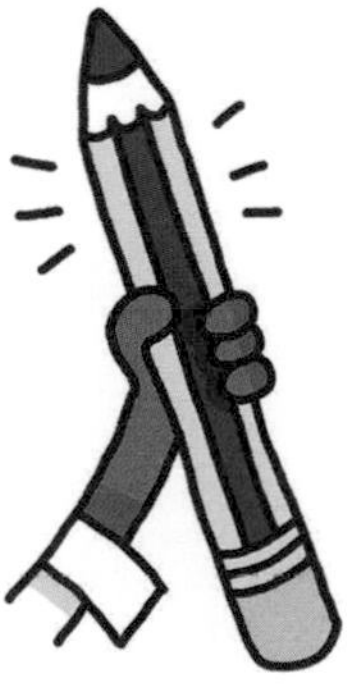

"Wow, look at this!" I said.

"Never mind that thing! Run before that radiated rodent **WAKES UP!!**" shouted Mona.

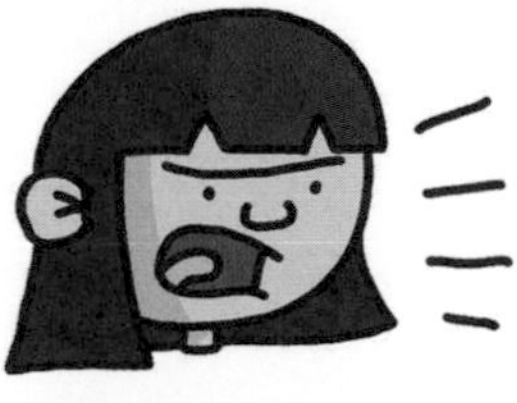

Chapter 3 **Escape from Fallout Island**

But when we reached the dock...

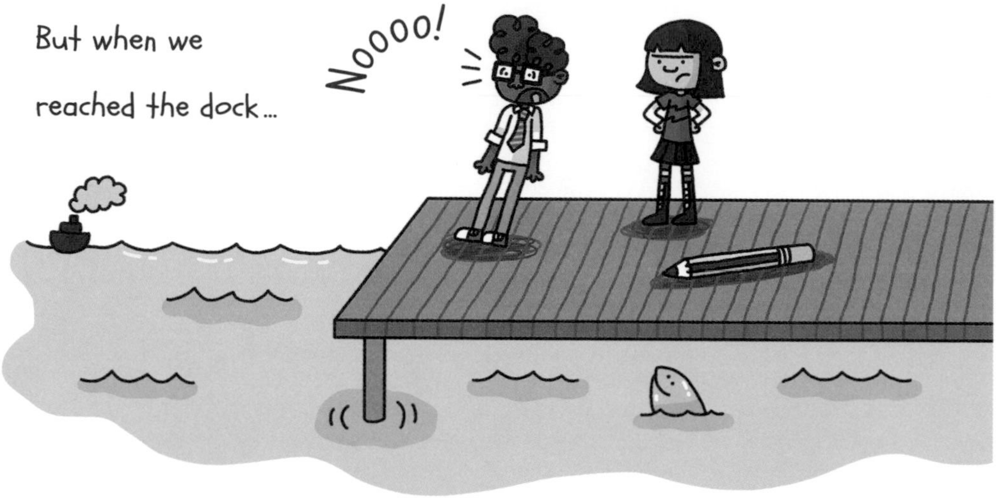
Noooo!

"NOOOO!" I shrieked.

"They left without us! I don't believe this! Trapped on a radioactive island with a mutant squirrel! GASP! Maybe we'll mutate too!"

Mona sighed. "Oh, CALM DOWN! We just need to think logically about this. Here's your stupid giant pencil!"

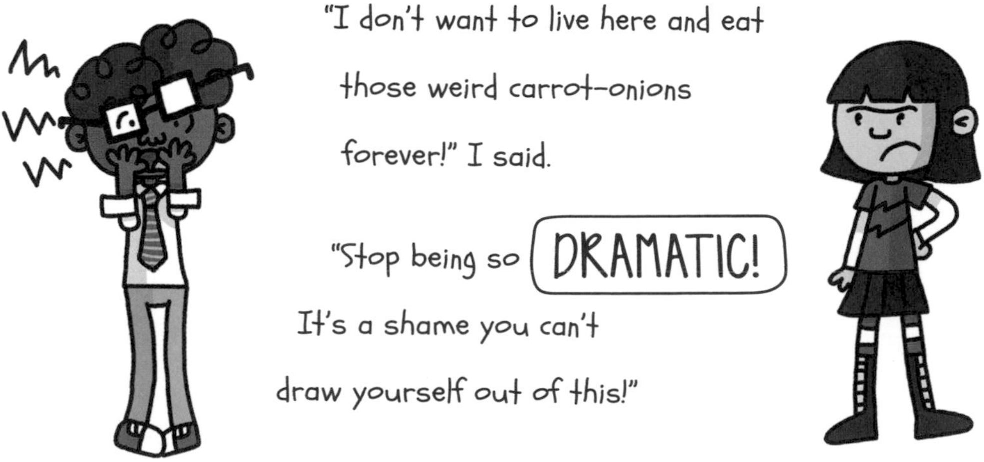

"I don't want to live here and eat those weird carrot-onions forever!" I said.

"Stop being so DRAMATIC! It's a shame you can't draw yourself out of this!"

"Hmm, maybe I CAN!"

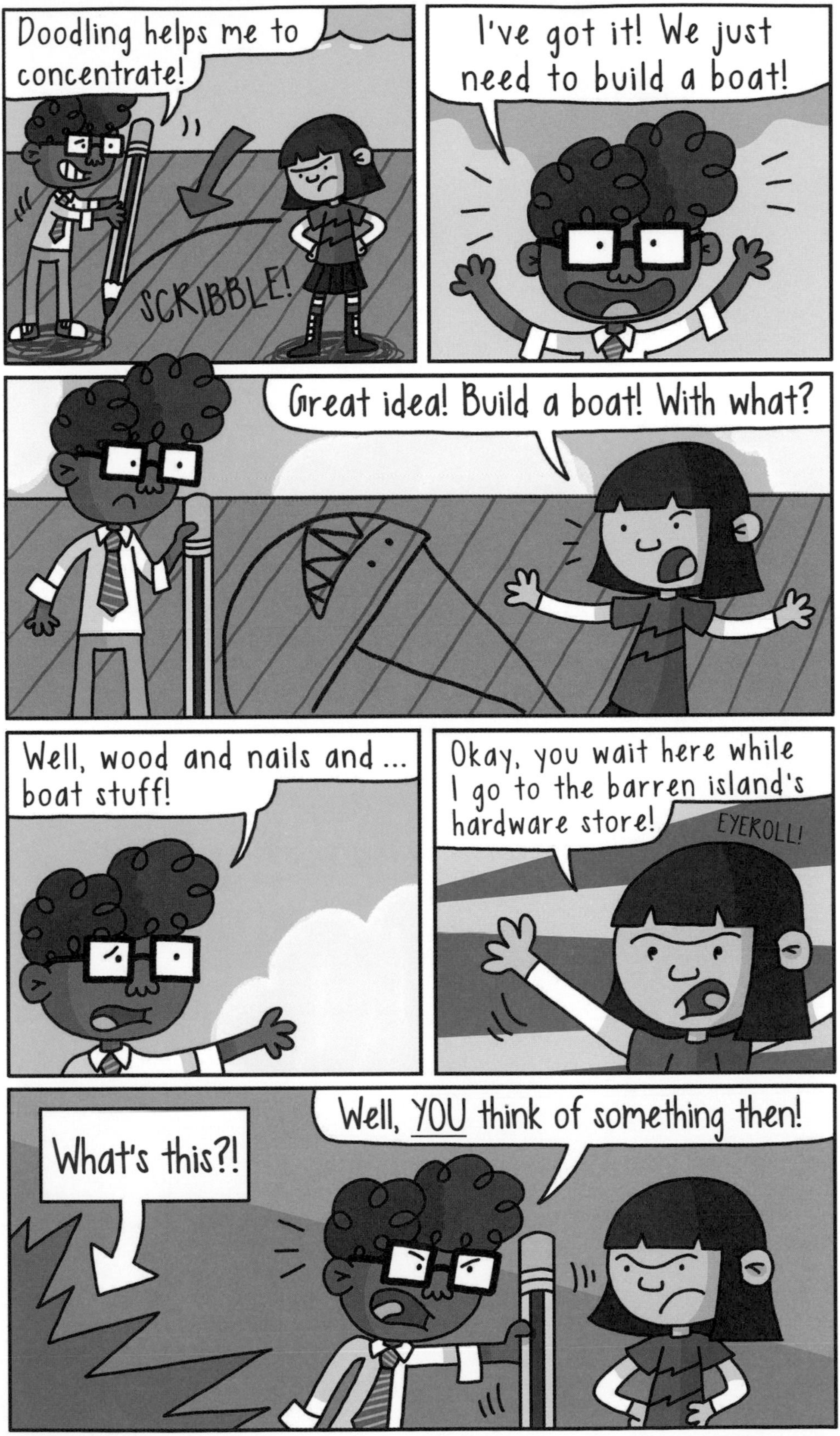
Doodling helps me to concentrate!
SCRIBBLE!
I've got it! We just need to build a boat!
Great idea! Build a boat! With what?
Well, wood and nails and ... boat stuff!
Okay, you wait here while I go to the barren island's hardware store!
EYEROLL!
Well, YOU think of something then!
What's this?!

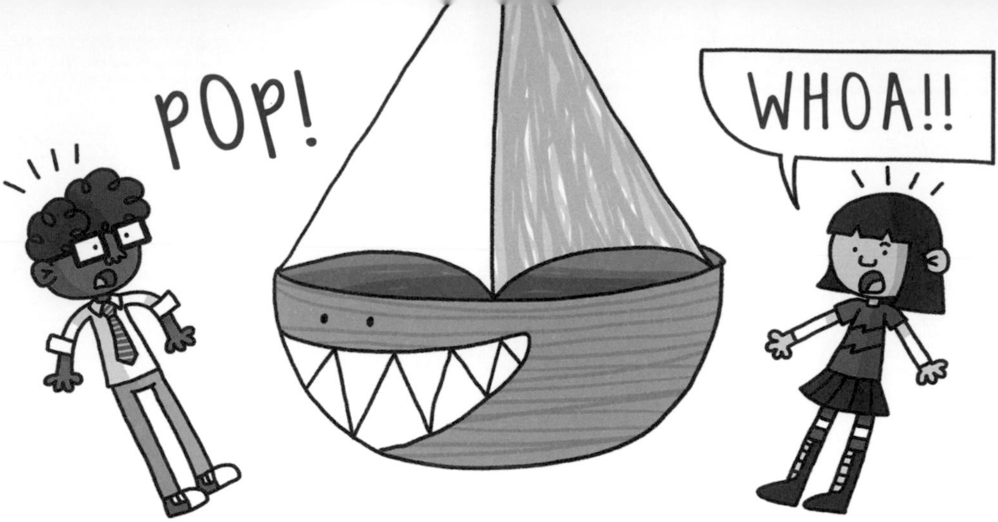
POP!
WHOA!!

The boat I had drawn CAME TO LIFE!

Mona poked it. "It's real!" she said. "Wow, I take back all of my sarcasm! The blootonium must have done something to your pencil!"

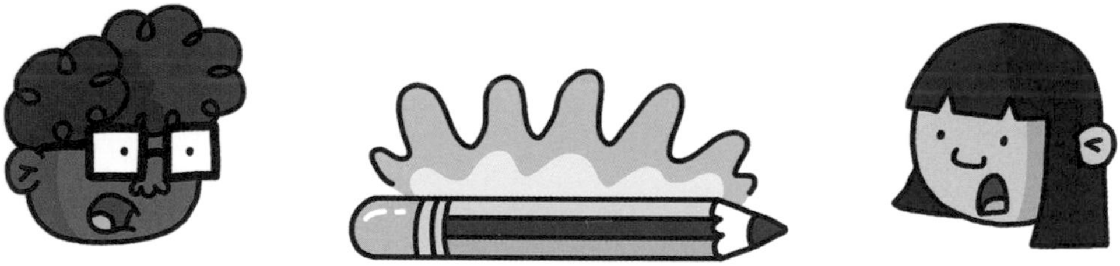

Just then, the monster reappeared.

"Oh no, Squirrelzilla woke up and now he looks even ANGRIER! We have to go!" I said.

"I think he wants your pencil," said Mona.

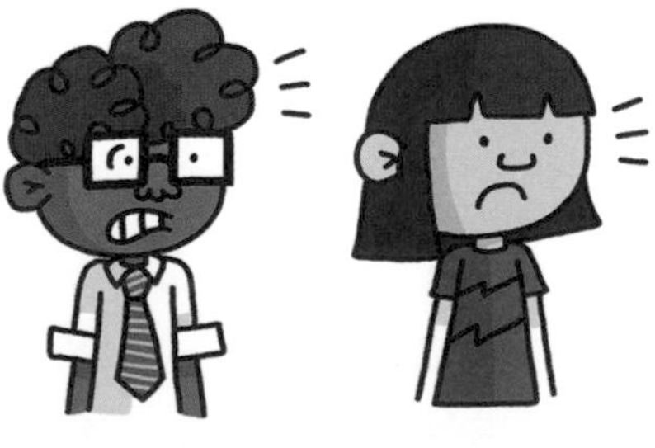

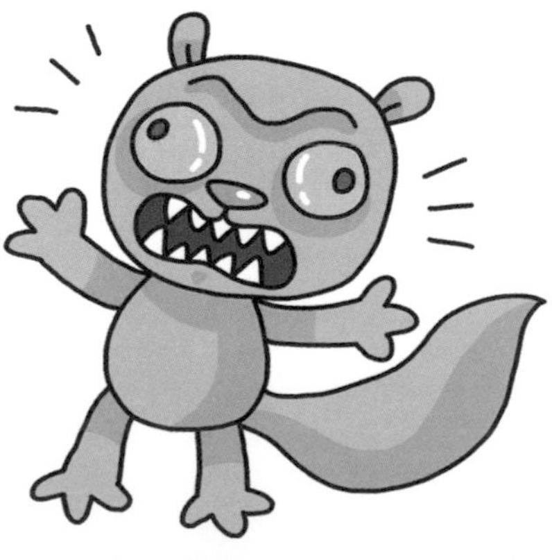

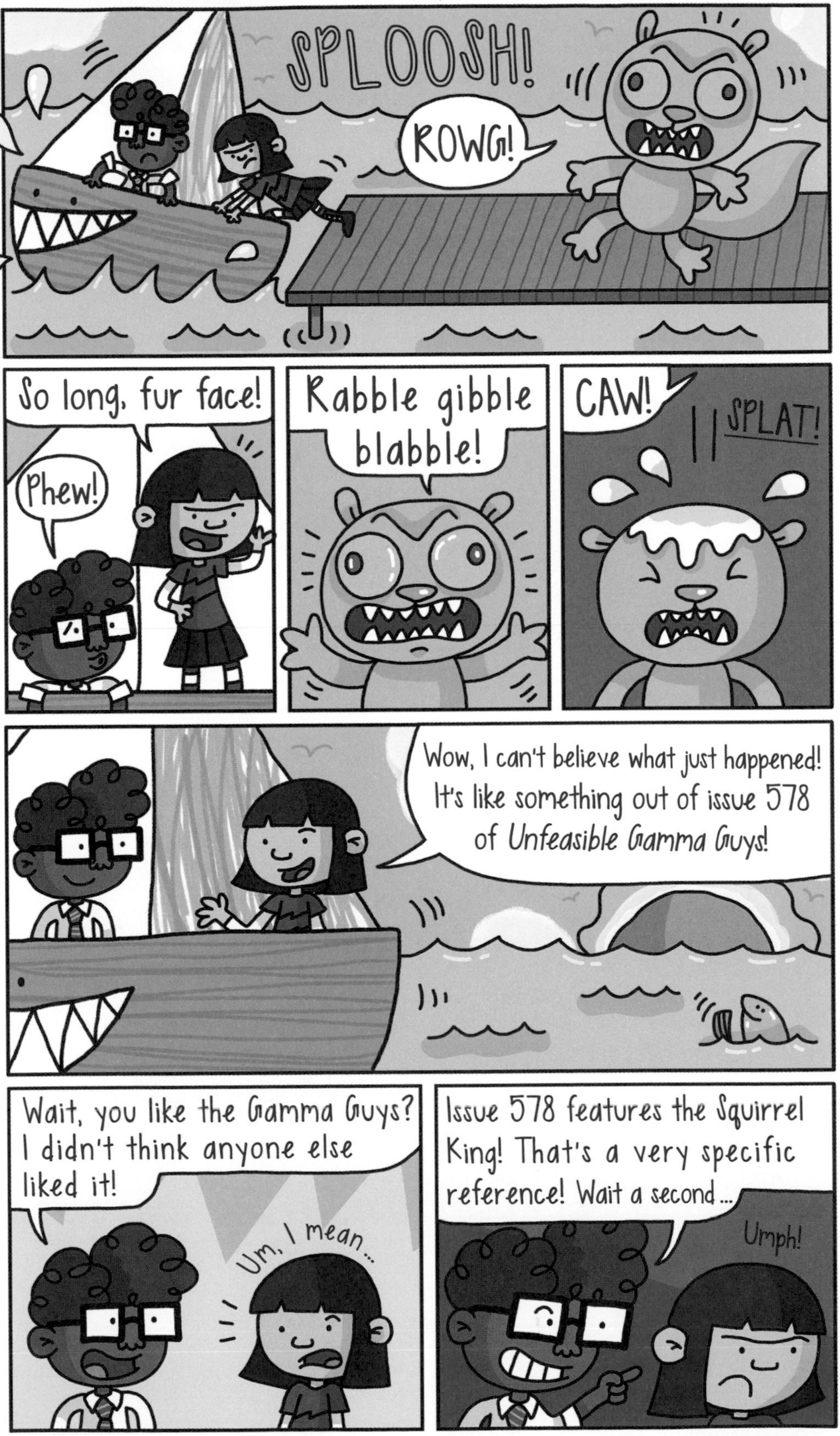
SPLOOSH!
ROWG!
So long, fur face!
Phew!
Rabble gibble blabble!
CAW!
SPLAT!
Wow, I can't believe what just happened! It's like something out of issue 578 of *Unfeasible Gamma Guys*!
Wait, you like the Gamma Guys? I didn't think anyone else liked it!
Um, I mean...
Issue 578 features the Squirrel King! That's a very specific reference! Wait a second...
Umph!

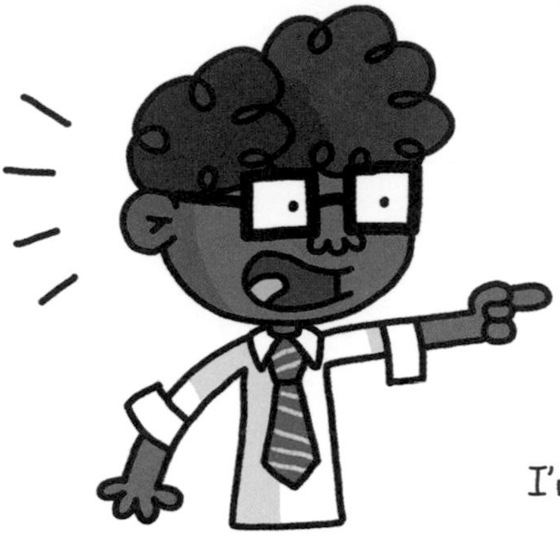

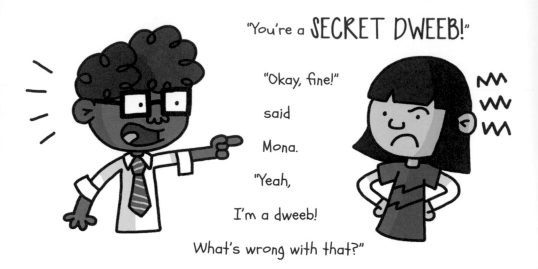

"You're a SECRET DWEEB!"

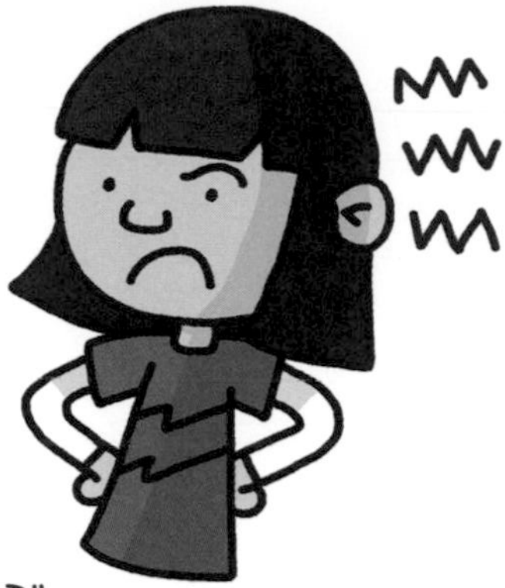

"Okay, fine!" said Mona. "Yeah, I'm a dweeb! What's wrong with that?"

"Nothing at all! EVERYONE should be a dweeb!" I replied.

Mona quickly changed the subject. "We should talk about this pencil and this boat. Will it get us back to the mainland?"

"I guess we'll find out," I said.

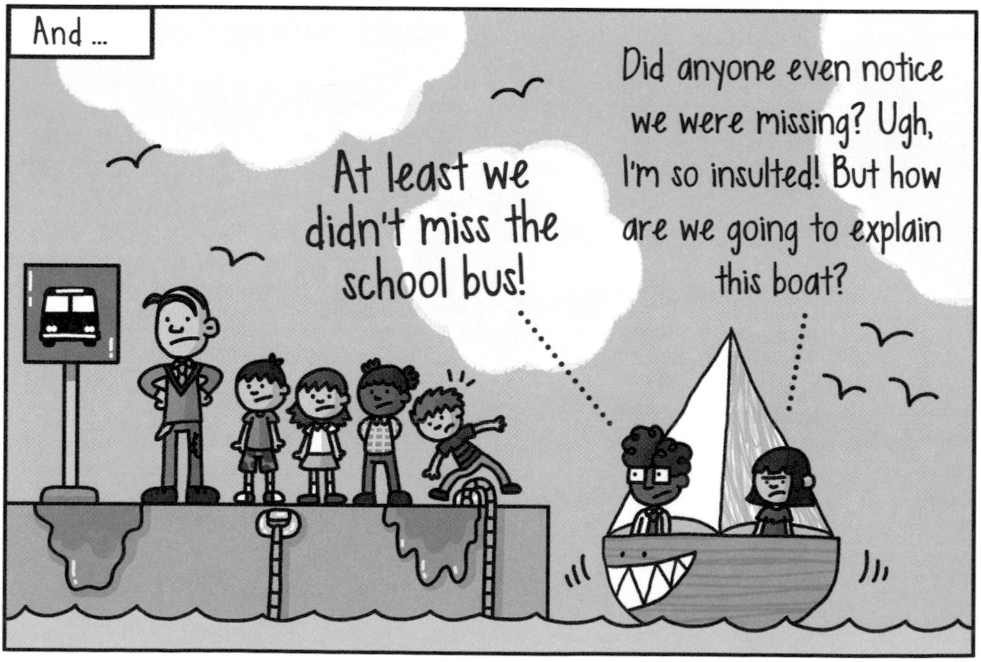
And ...
At least we didn't miss the school bus!
Did anyone even notice we were missing? Ugh, I'm so insulted! But how are we going to explain this boat?

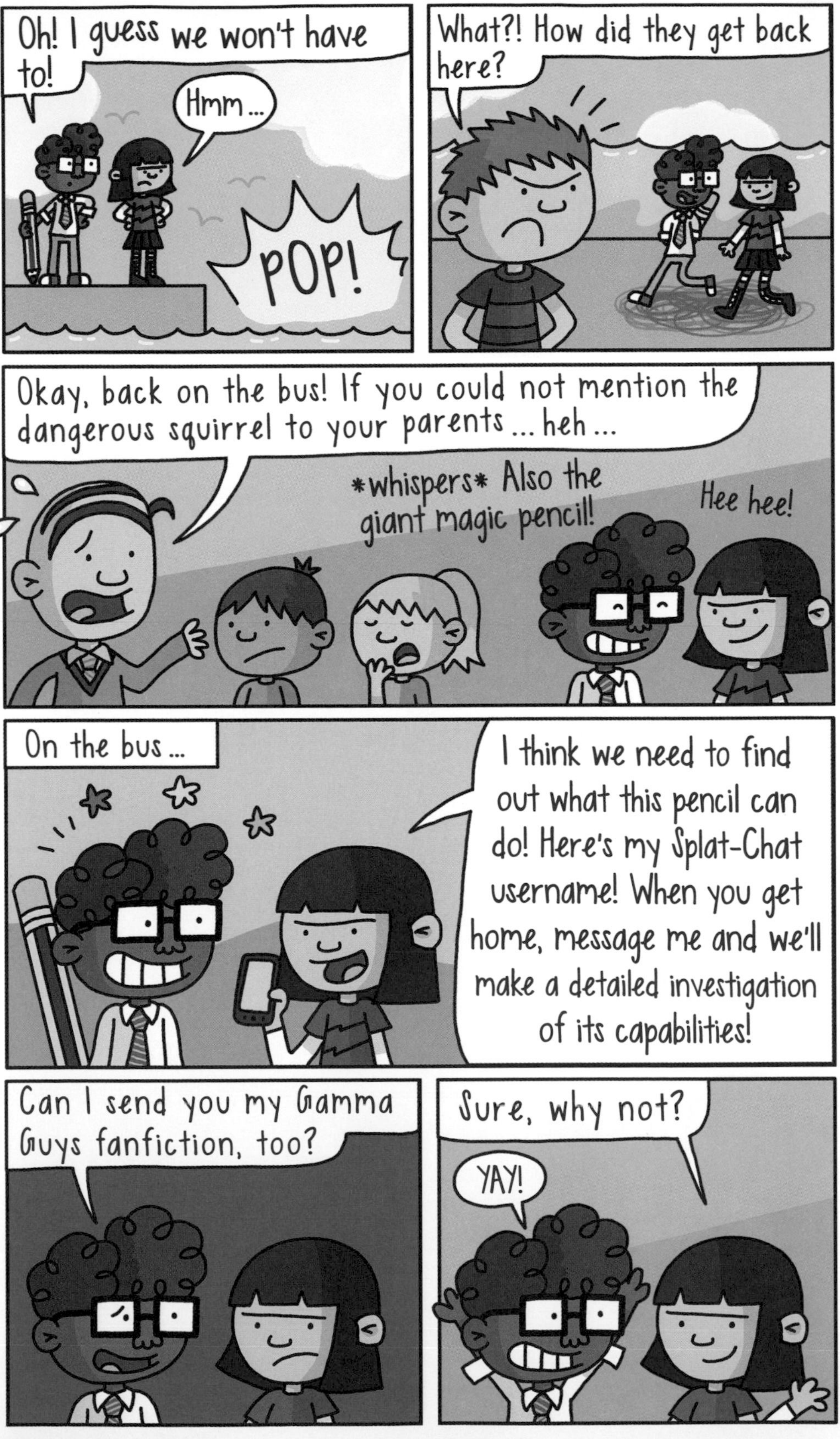
Oh! I guess we won't have to!
Hmm ...
POP!
What?! How did they get back here?
Okay, back on the bus! If you could not mention the dangerous squirrel to your parents ... heh ...
whispers Also the giant magic pencil!
Hee hee!
On the bus ...
I think we need to find out what this pencil can do! Here's my Splat-Chat username! When you get home, message me and we'll make a detailed investigation of its capabilities!
Can I send you my Gamma Guys fanfiction, too?
Sure, why not?
YAY!

During dinner, all I could think about was testing out my new pencil!

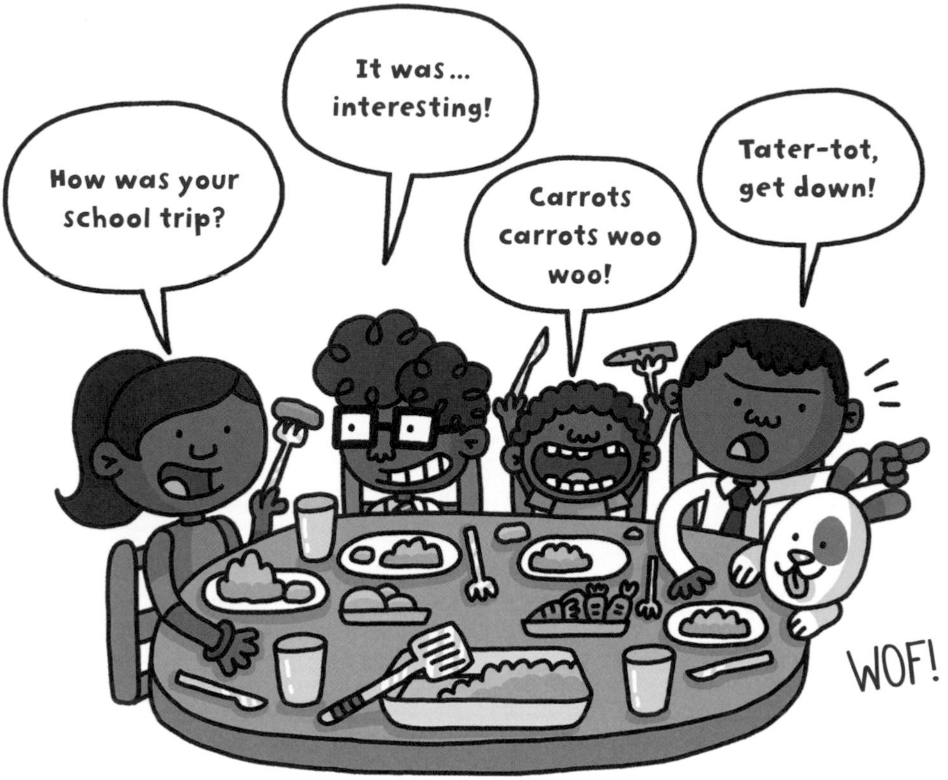
How was your school trip?
It was... interesting!
Carrots carrots woo woo!
Tater-tot, get down!
WOF!

I wolfed down everything and headed to my room. "Finished! I'm off to do my *HOMEWORK!*"

"Dishes first," said Mom. Argh! "But my homework!" I whined.

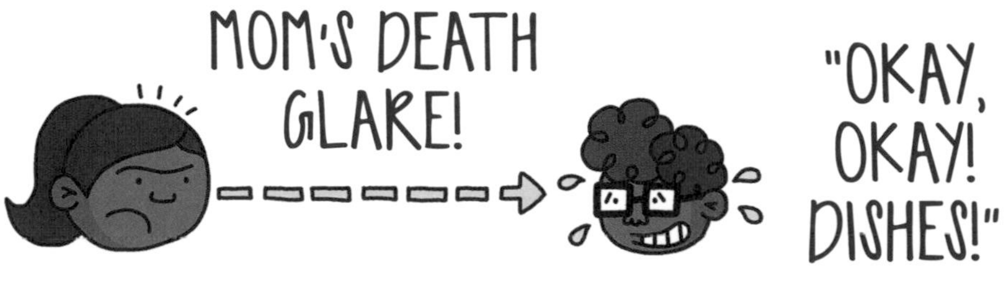
MOM'S DEATH GLARE!
"OKAY, OKAY! DISHES!"

FINALLY, after the dishes were done, I raced to my room! "Come on, Taters!"

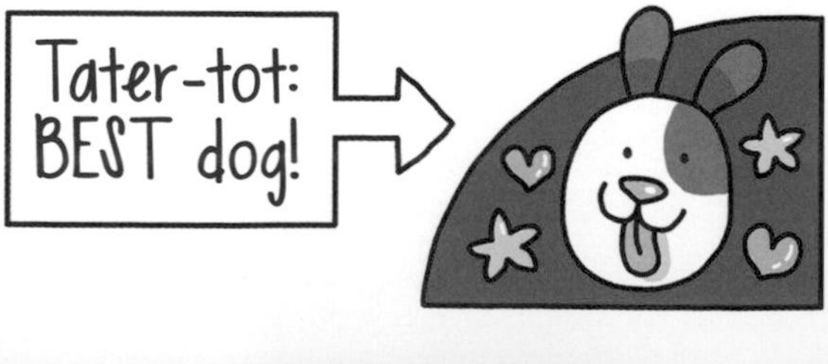
Tater-tot: BEST dog!

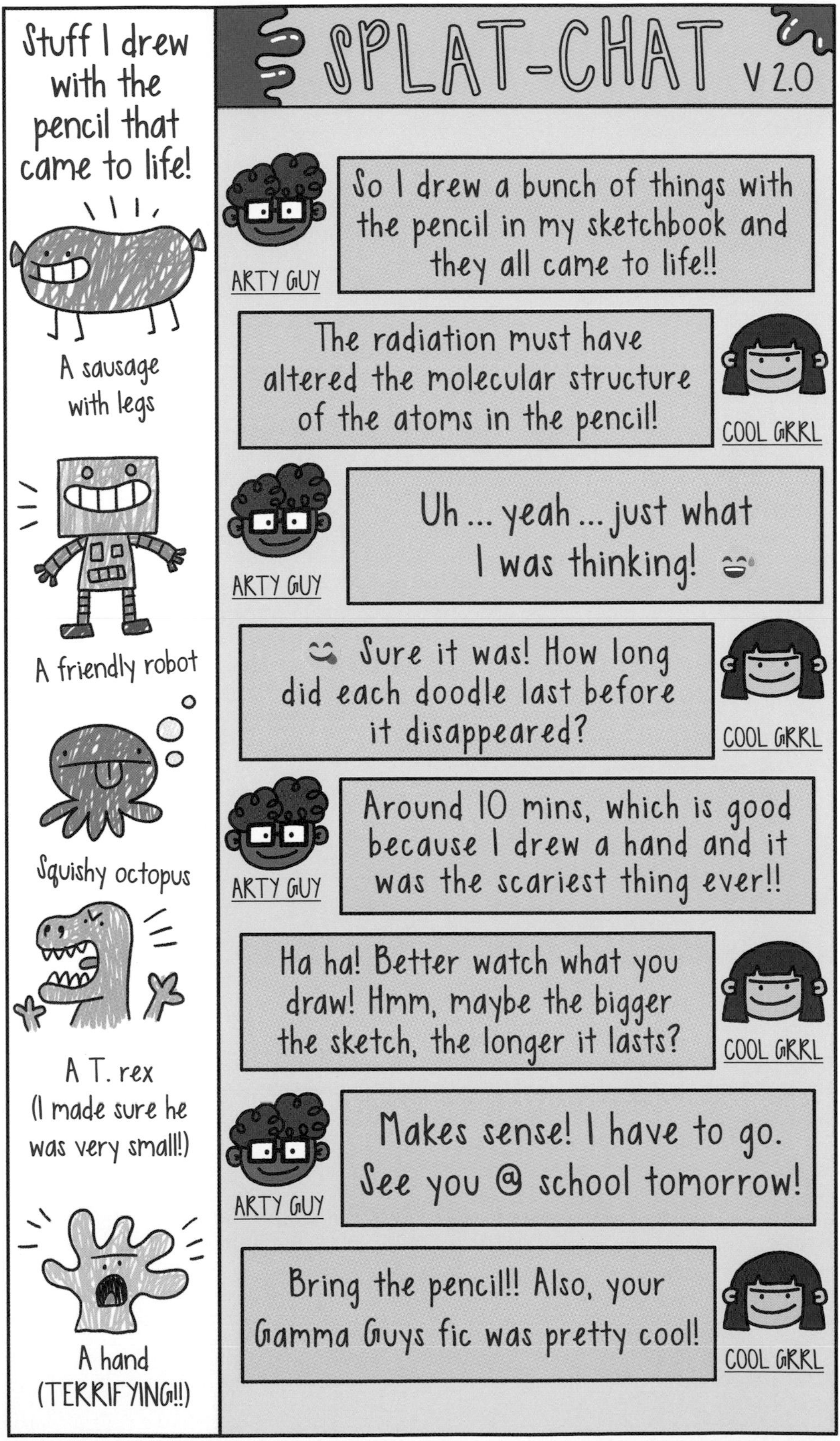
Stuff I drew with the pencil that came to life!
A sausage with legs
A friendly robot
Squishy octopus
A T. rex (I made sure he was very small!)
A hand (TERRIFYING!!)
SPLAT-CHAT V 2.0
ARTY GUY
So I drew a bunch of things with the pencil in my sketchbook and they all came to life!!
The radiation must have altered the molecular structure of the atoms in the pencil!
COOL GRRL
ARTY GUY
Uh ... yeah ... just what I was thinking!
Sure it was! How long did each doodle last before it disappeared?
COOL GRRL
ARTY GUY
Around 10 mins, which is good because I drew a hand and it was the scariest thing ever!!
Ha ha! Better watch what you draw! Hmm, maybe the bigger the sketch, the longer it lasts?
COOL GRRL
ARTY GUY
Makes sense! I have to go. See you @ school tomorrow!
Bring the pencil!! Also, your Gamma Guys fic was pretty cool!
COOL GRRL

Chapter 4 **Pencil Power!**

The next morning ...

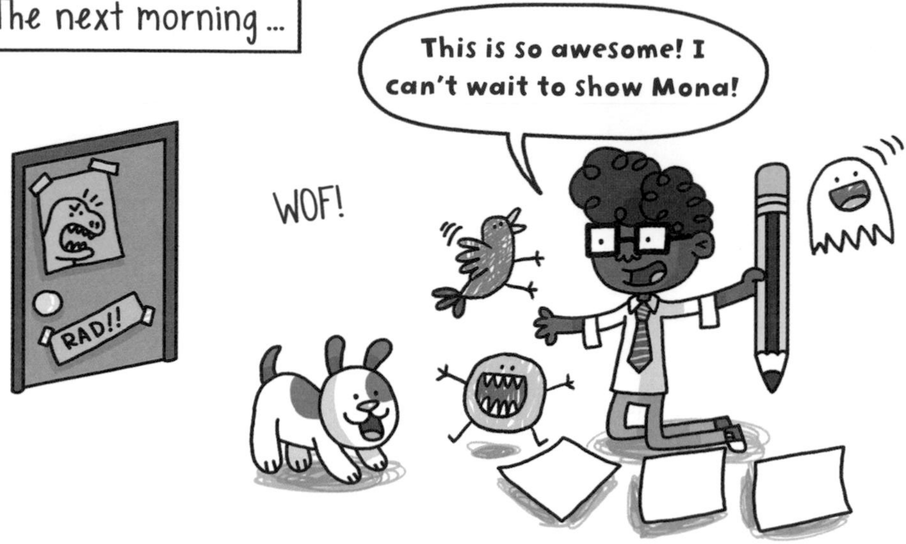
This is so awesome! I can't wait to show Mona!
WOF!
RAD!!

Of course, living with a little brother is a risk to magic pencil security ...

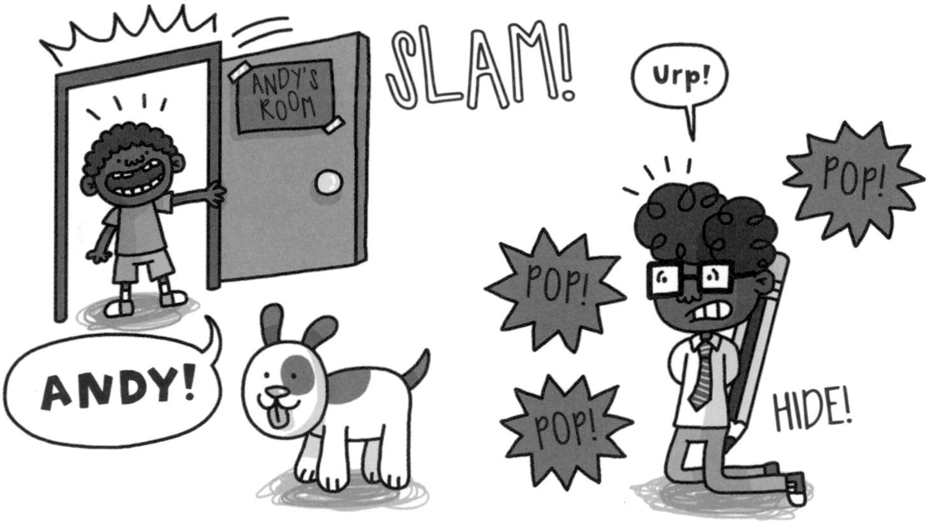
ANDY'S ROOM
SLAM!
Urp!
POP!
POP!
POP!
ANDY!
HIDE!

"What have you got?" Oscar asked.

"NOTHING! It's a ... project for school!" I said hastily.

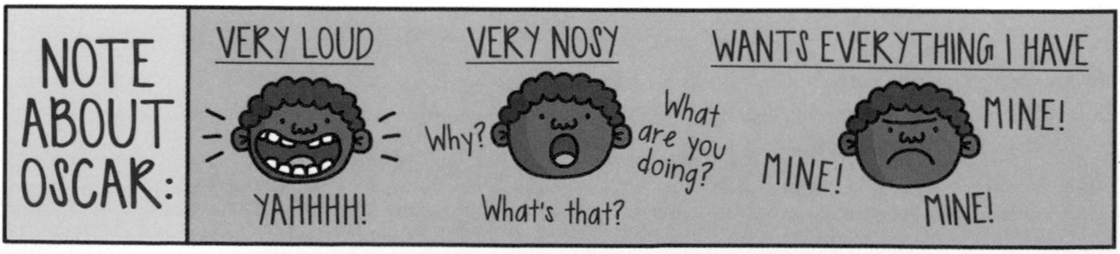
NOTE ABOUT OSCAR:
VERY LOUD
YAHHHH!
VERY NOSY
Why?
What are you doing?
What's that?
WANTS EVERYTHING I HAVE
MINE!
MINE!
MINE!

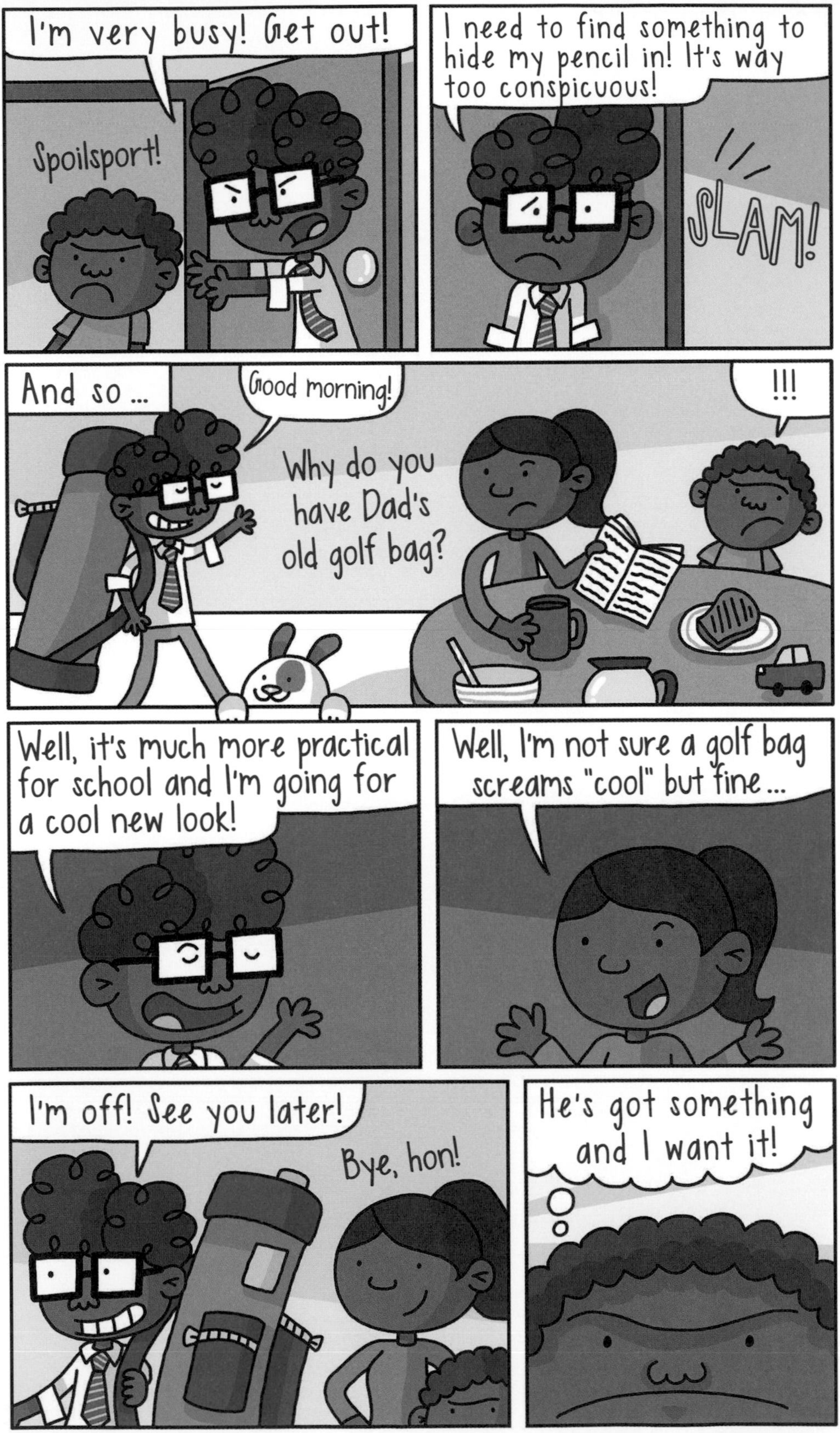
I'm very busy! Get out!
Spoilsport!
I need to find something to hide my pencil in! It's way too conspicuous!
SLAM!
And so ...
Good morning!
Why do you have Dad's old golf bag?
!!!
Well, it's much more practical for school and I'm going for a cool new look!
Well, I'm not sure a golf bag screams "cool" but fine ...
I'm off! See you later!
Bye, hon!
He's got something and I want it!

I knew I'd get some funny looks at the bus stop but I didn't care—I had a magic pencil!

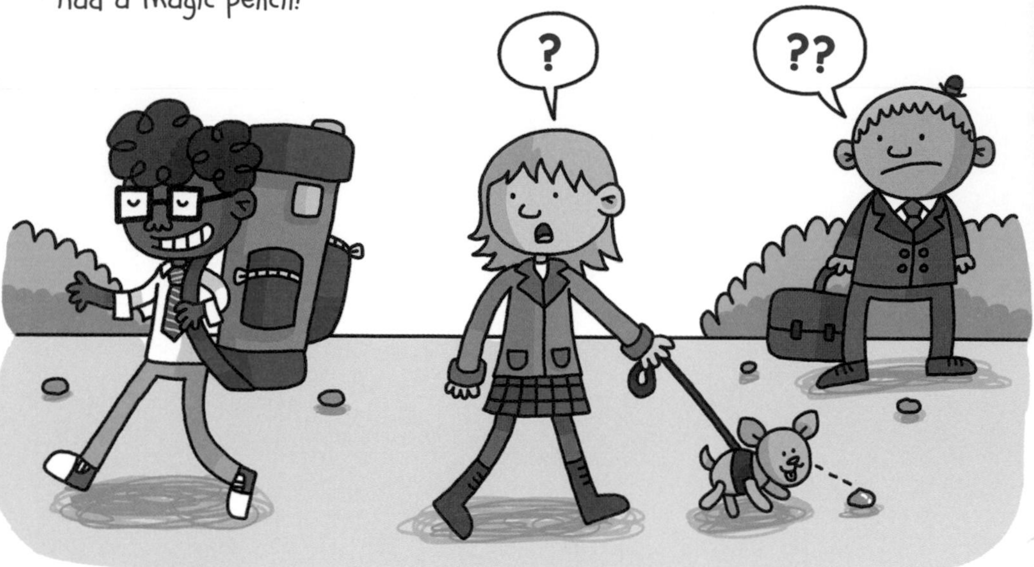
?
??

I messaged Mona when I got on the bus ...

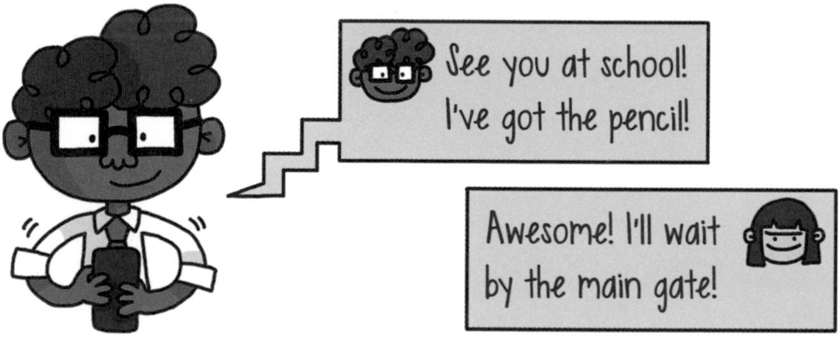
See you at school! I've got the pencil!
Awesome! I'll wait by the main gate!

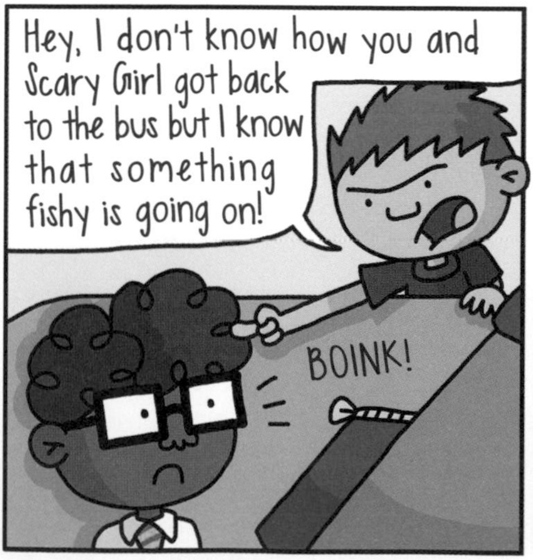
Hey, I don't know how you and Scary Girl got back to the bus but I know that something fishy is going on!
BOINK!

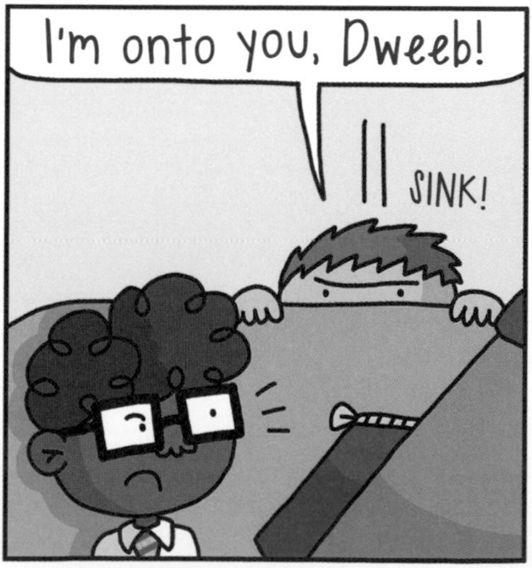
I'm onto you, Dweeb!
SINK!

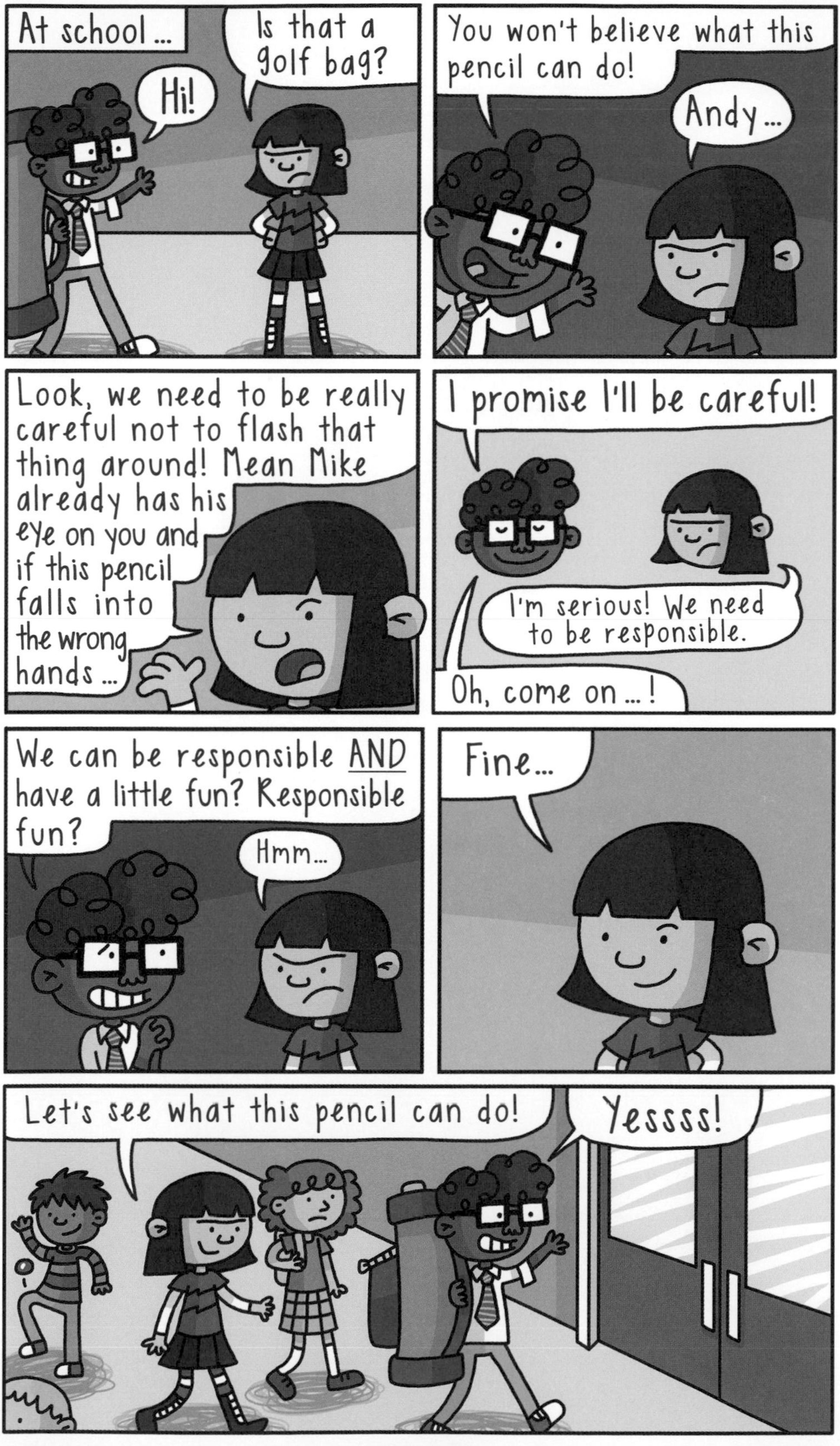
At school ...
Hi!
Is that a golf bag?
You won't believe what this pencil can do!
Andy ...
Look, we need to be really careful not to flash that thing around! Mean Mike already has his eye on you and if this pencil falls into the wrong hands ...
I promise I'll be careful!
I'm serious! We need to be responsible.
Oh, come on ... !
We can be responsible AND have a little fun? Responsible fun?
Hmm...
Fine...
Let's see what this pencil can do!
Yessss!

As soon as we got into class ...

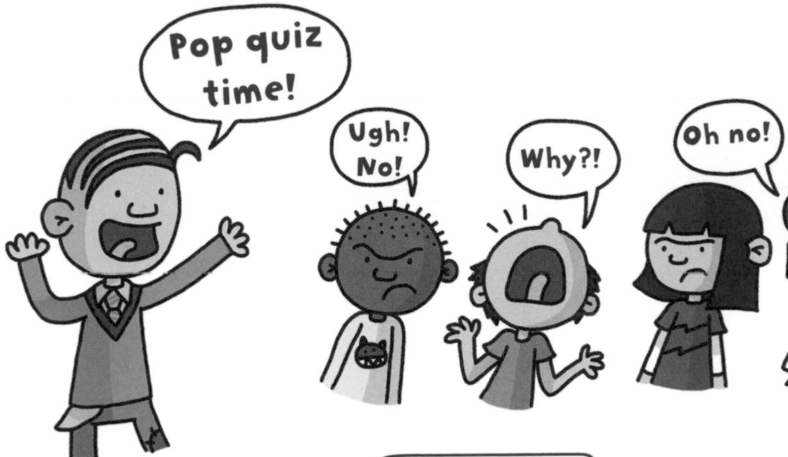
Pop quiz time!
Ugh! No!
Why?!
Oh no!

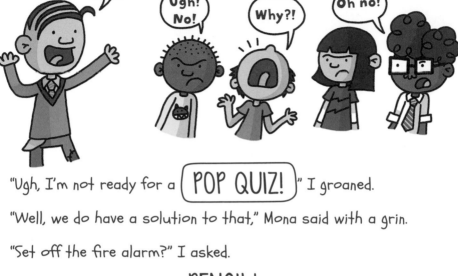

"Ugh, I'm not ready for a POP QUIZ!" I groaned.

"Well, we do have a solution to that," Mona said with a grin.

"Set off the fire alarm?" I asked.

Mona rolled her eyes. "The PENCIL!"

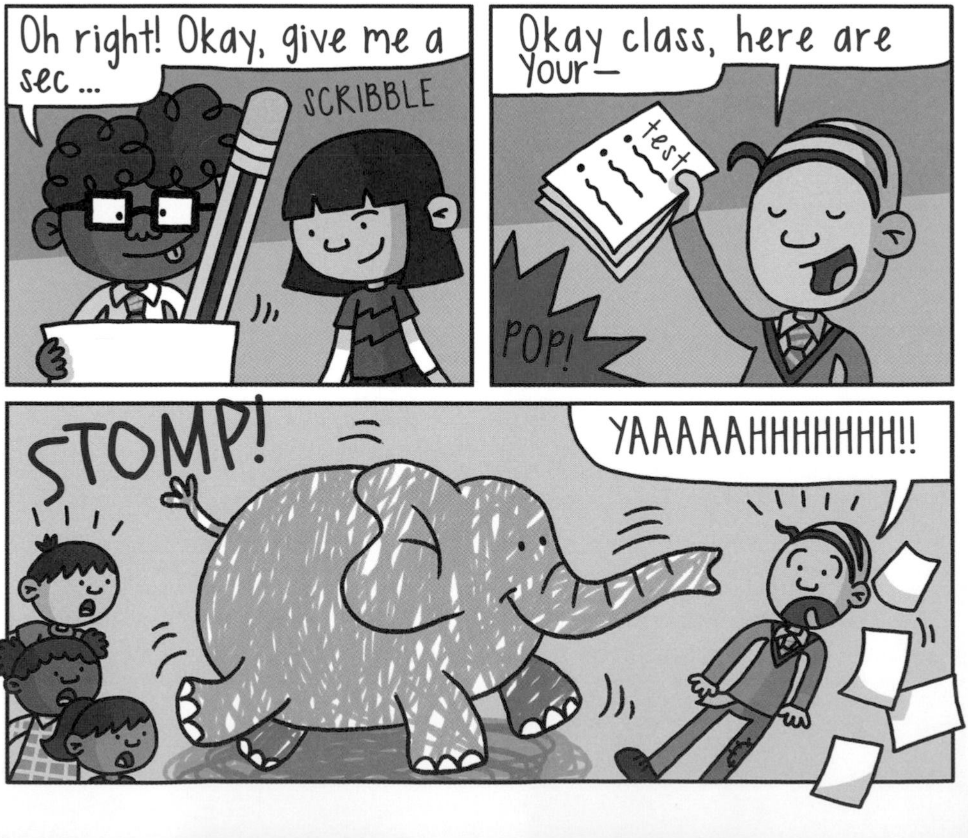
Oh right! Okay, give me a sec ...
SCRIBBLE
Okay class, here are your—
test
POP!
STOMP!
YAAAAAHHHHHHH!!

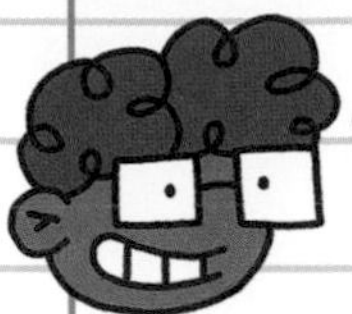

FUN WE HAD WITH THE PENCIL!

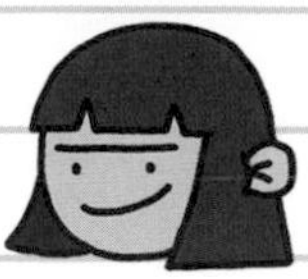

Drawing a gang of raccoons to chase Mean Mike and his goons!

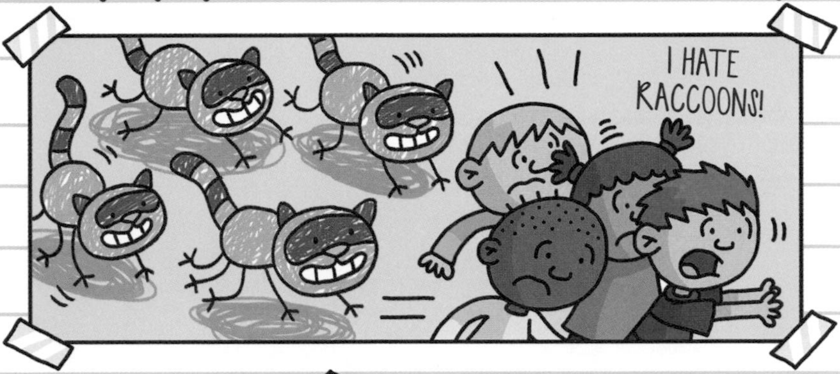
I HATE RACCOONS!

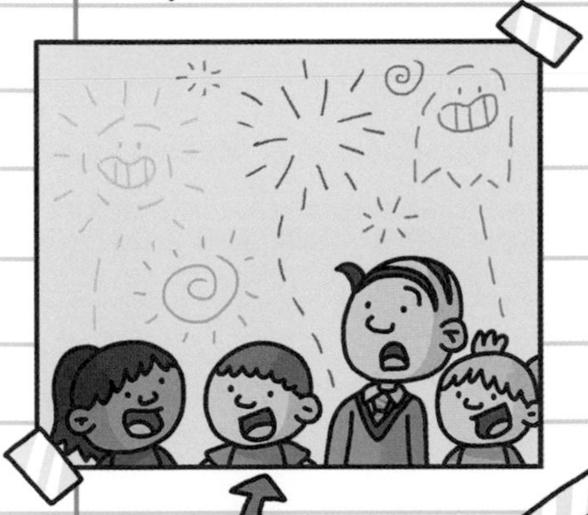

FIREWORK DISPLAY!

ENTERTAINING THE SCHOOL WITH A GIANT DANCING PINEAPPLE!

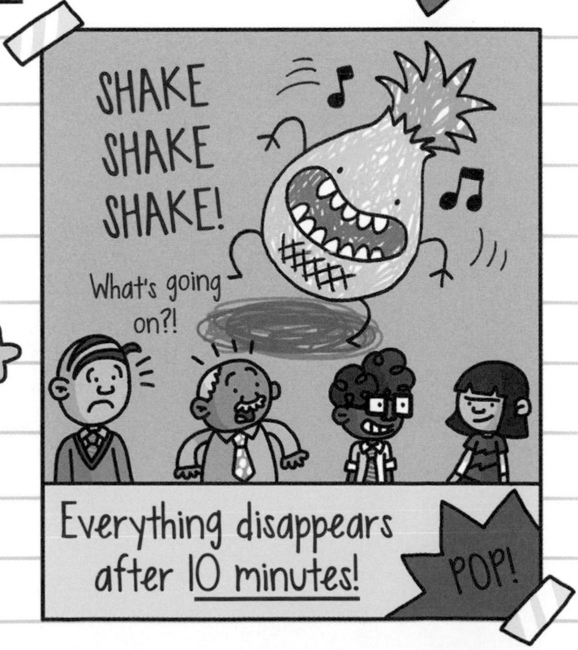
SHAKE
SHAKE
SHAKE!
What's going on?!
Everything disappears after 10 minutes!
POP!

THIS PENCIL IS ...

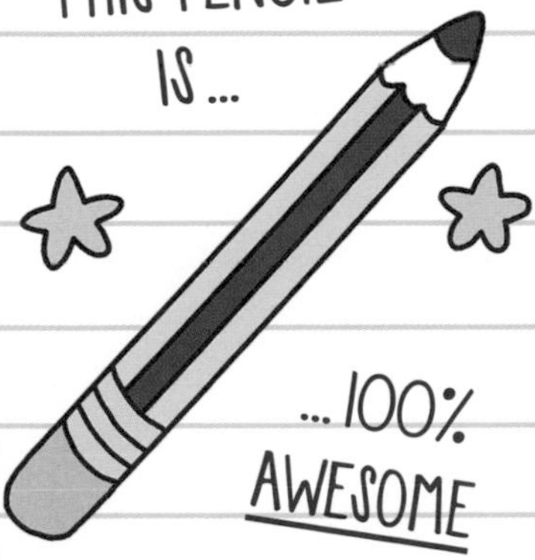

... 100% AWESOME

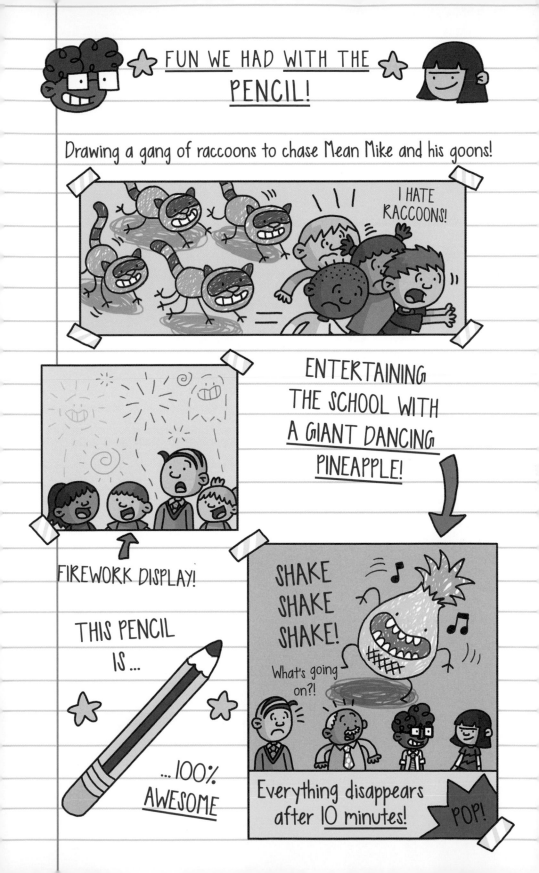

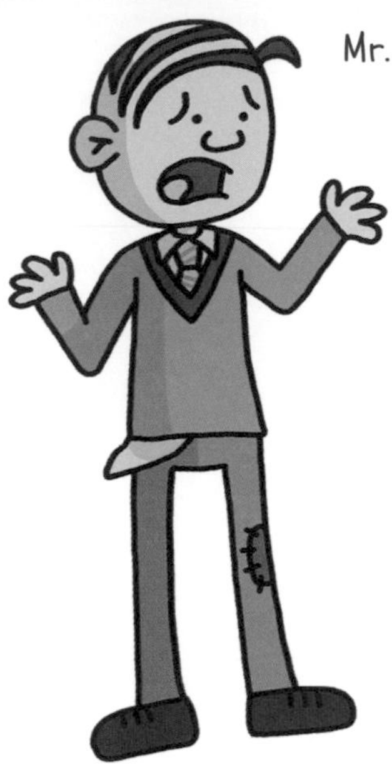

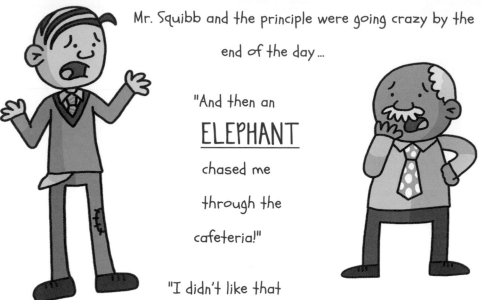

Mr. Squibb and the principle were going crazy by the end of the day ...

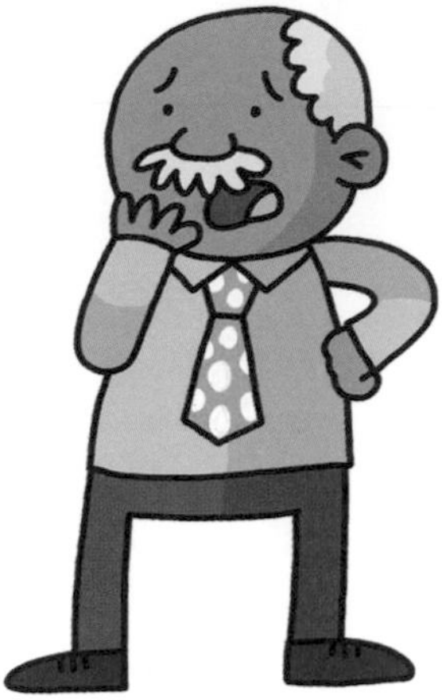

"And then an **ELEPHANT** chased me through the cafeteria!"

"I didn't like that **DANCING PINEAPPLE** one bit!"

Everyone was talking about it! I felt like I had the best secret in the world. Mona wasn't as enthusiastic about it though ...

"Okay, today has been fun and all but we really can't do anything like this again," she said.

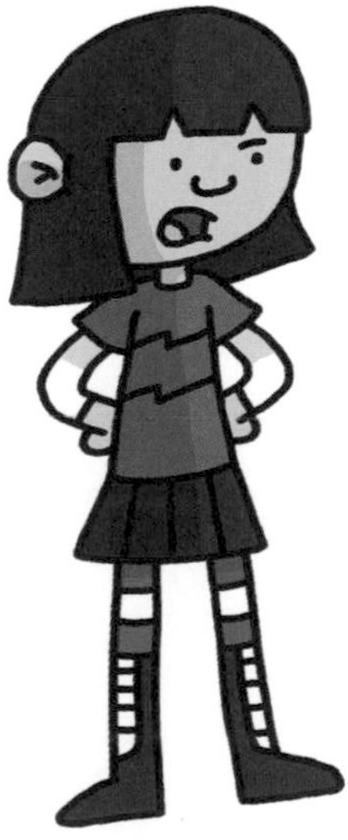

"Oh, you worry too much! What could **POSSIBLY** go wrong with a **MAGIC PENCIL** that makes art come to life?"

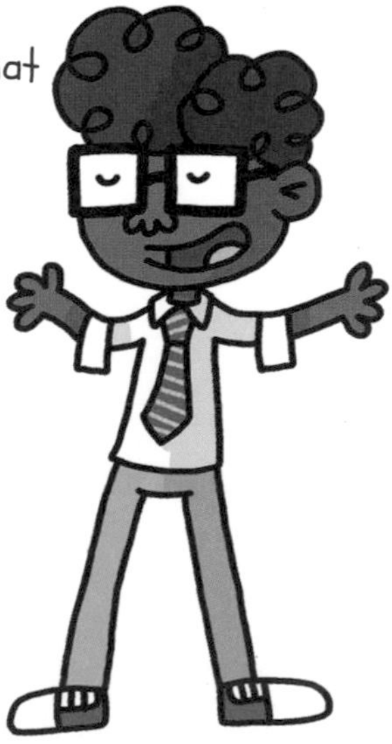

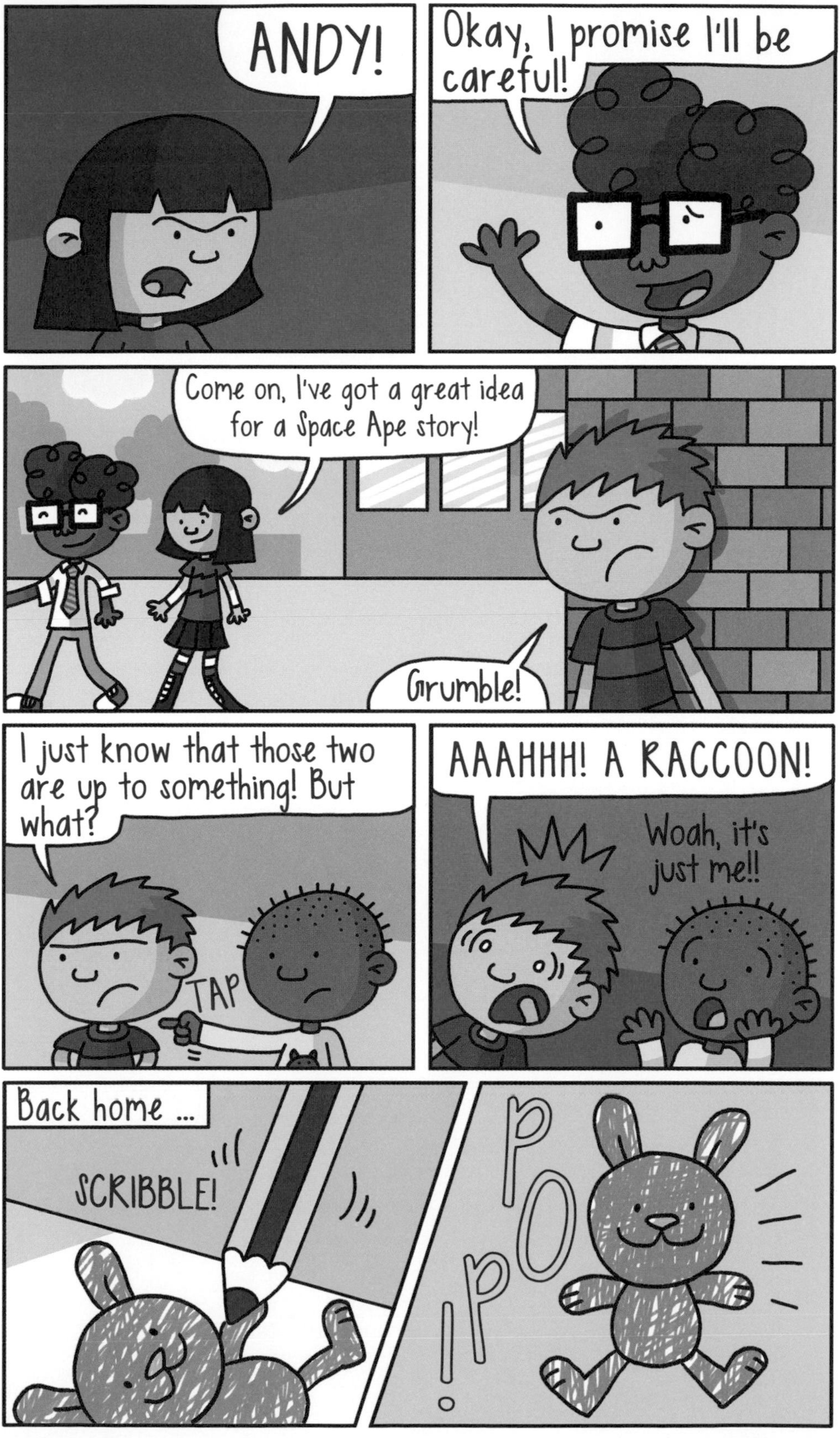
ANDY!
Okay, I promise I'll be careful!
Come on, I've got a great idea for a Space Ape story!
Grumble!
I just know that those two are up to something! But what?
TAP
AAAHHH! A RACCOON!
Woah, it's just me!!
Back home ...
SCRIBBLE!
POP!

"This is so much fun! I love this pencil!"

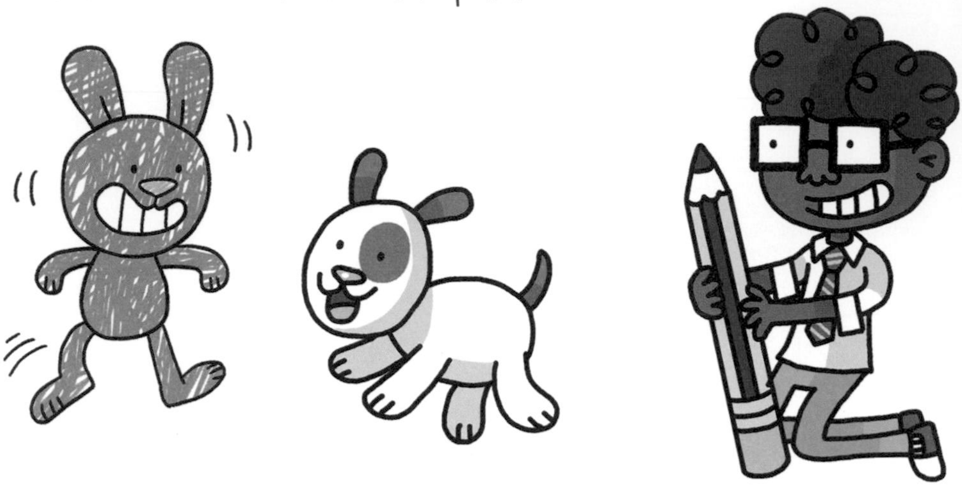

Things were looking

so SWEET right now! Anything was

possible with this pencil. Maybe I could run for student president!

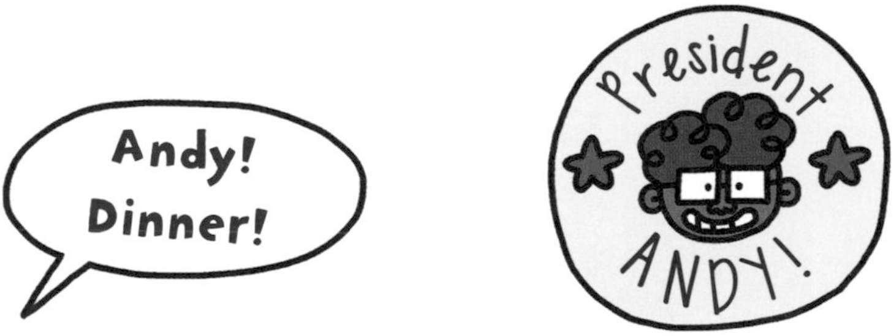
Andy! Dinner!
President
ANDY!

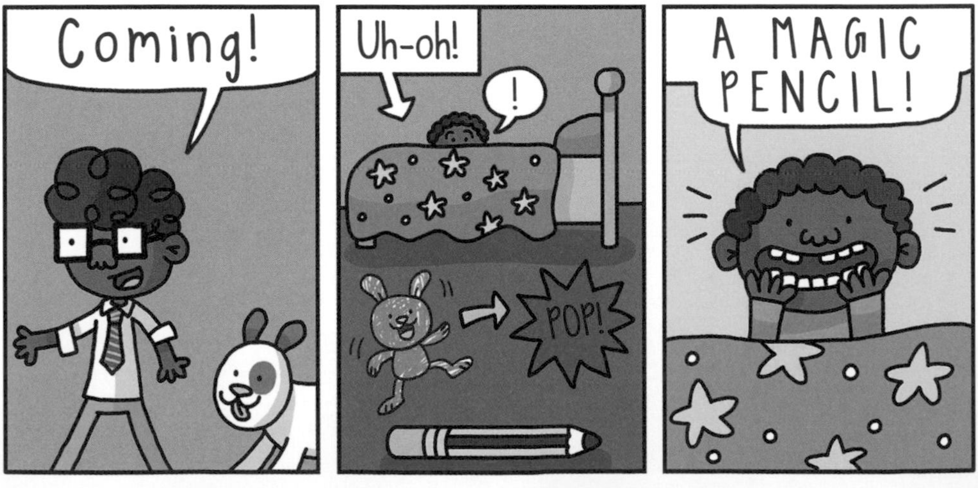
Coming!
Uh-oh!
!
POP!
A MAGIC PENCIL!

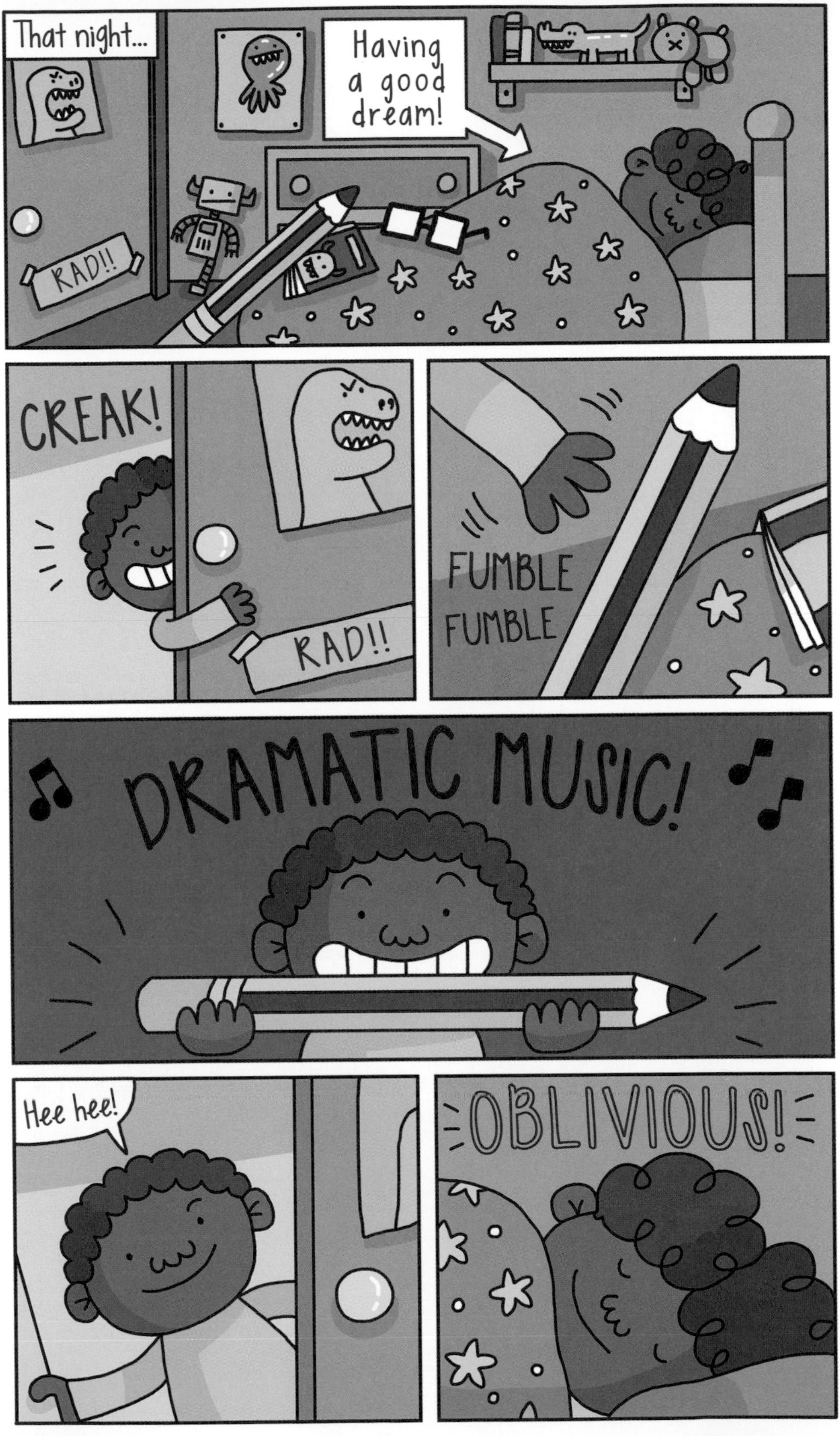
That night...
Having a good dream!
RAD!!
CREAK!
RAD!!
FUMBLE
FUMBLE
DRAMATIC MUSIC!
Hee hee!
OBLIVIOUS!

Chapter 5 The Scribble Monster

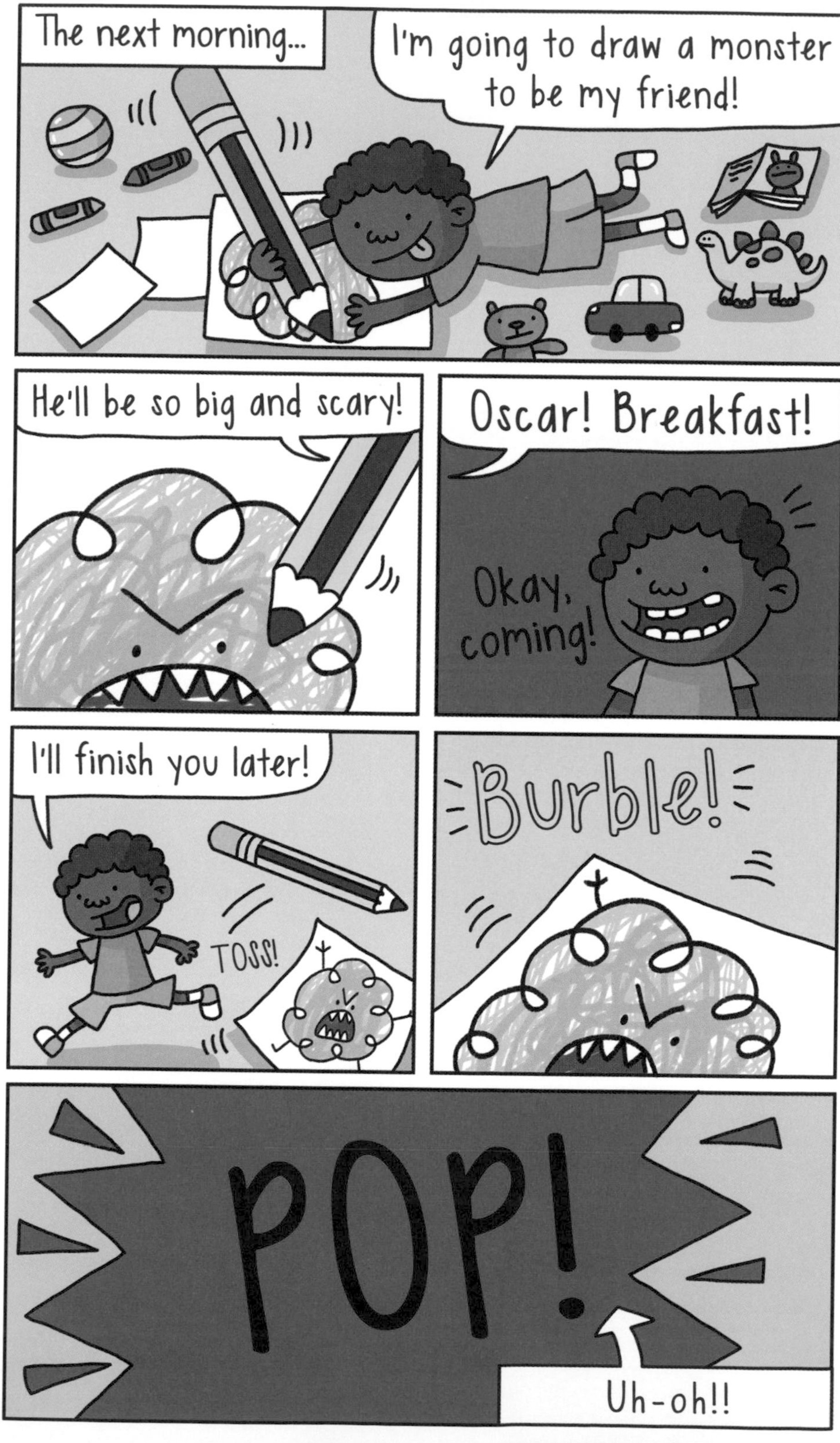

The next morning...
I'm going to draw a monster to be my friend!
He'll be so big and scary!
Oscar! Breakfast!
Okay, coming!
I'll finish you later!
TOSS!
Burble!
POP!
Uh-oh!!

I woke up feeling great! I couldn't wait
to do some more doodling!

BUT
WAIT.

Um, <u>WHERE'S MY PENCIL?</u>

I'm sure the pencil was right here!

GONE!

Okay, don't panic! It must just be under

my bed or in my closet...

But the pencil was GONE!

"Mona's going to be so totally unimpressed with

me! I'll   be hearing "I TOLD YOU SO" until the end of time!"

CRASH!

What
was that?!

It came from Oscar's
room!

Nice
jammies!

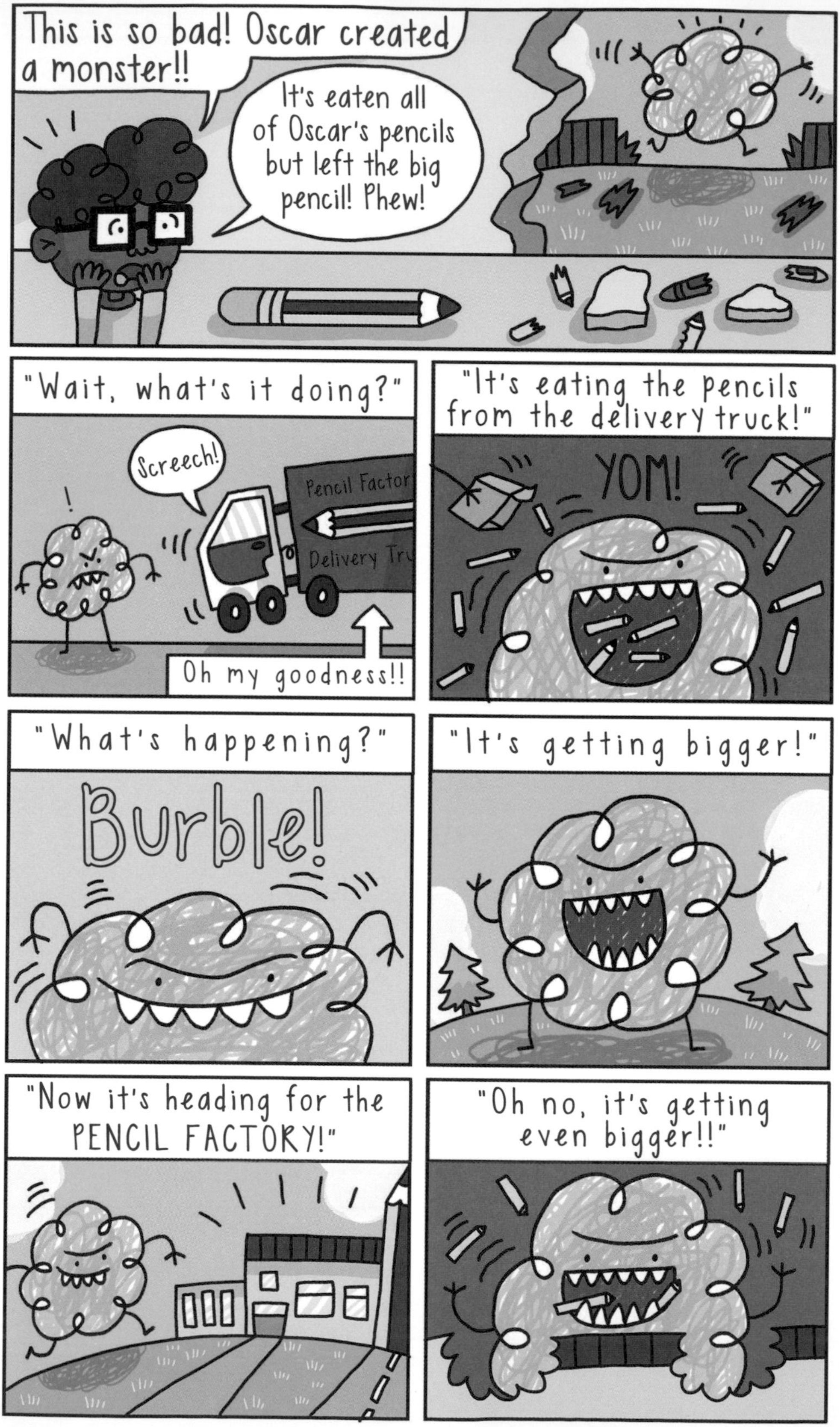
This is so bad! Oscar created a monster!!
It's eaten all of Oscar's pencils but left the big pencil! Phew!
"Wait, what's it doing?"
Screech!
Pencil Factor
Delivery Tru
Oh my goodness!!
"It's eating the pencils from the delivery truck!"
YOM!
"What's happening?"
Burble!
"It's getting bigger!"
"Now it's heading for the PENCIL FACTORY!"
"Oh no, it's getting even bigger!!"

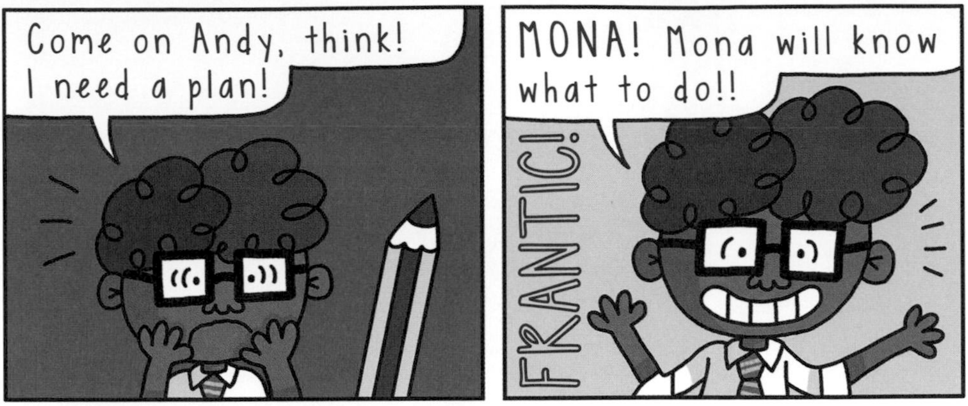
Come on Andy, think! I need a plan!
MONA! Mona will know what to do!!
FRANTIC!

"ANDY, BREAKFAST!" Mom called.

I quickly got dressed and grabbed the pencil. Running down the stairs, I pointed at Oscar.

"YOU!" I hissed.

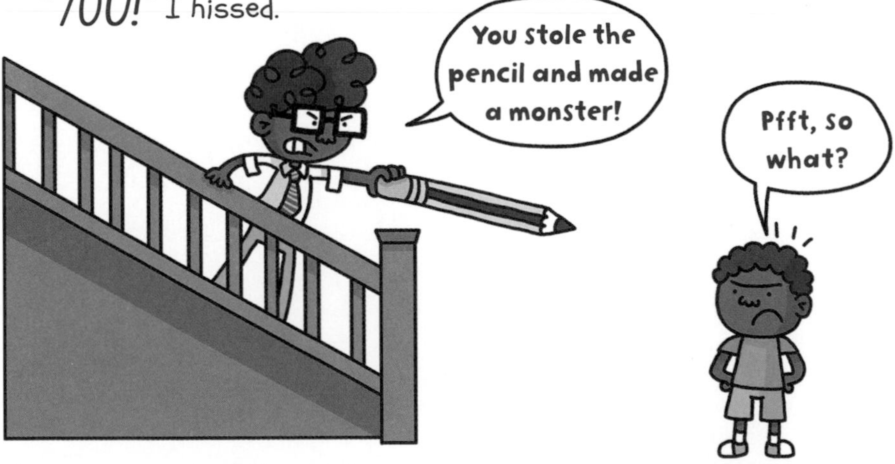
You stole the pencil and made a monster!
Pfft, so what?

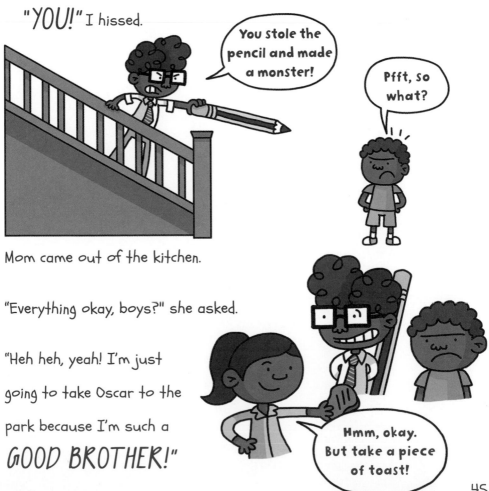

Mom came out of the kitchen.

"Everything okay, boys?" she asked.

"Heh heh, yeah! I'm just going to take Oscar to the park because I'm such a *GOOD BROTHER!*"

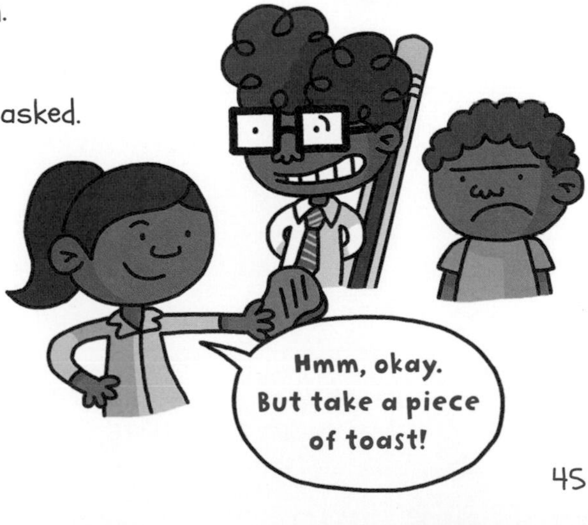
Hmm, okay. But take a piece of toast!

We raced out of the house and I told Oscar how much **TROUBLE** he had caused.

"This is terrible! I'm the one who's going to be grounded until I'm an old man! Never mind the hole in the side of our house!"

We **RAN** down the street and as we rounded a corner we ran into ...

Mean Mike and his gang! Ugh, this was all I needed!

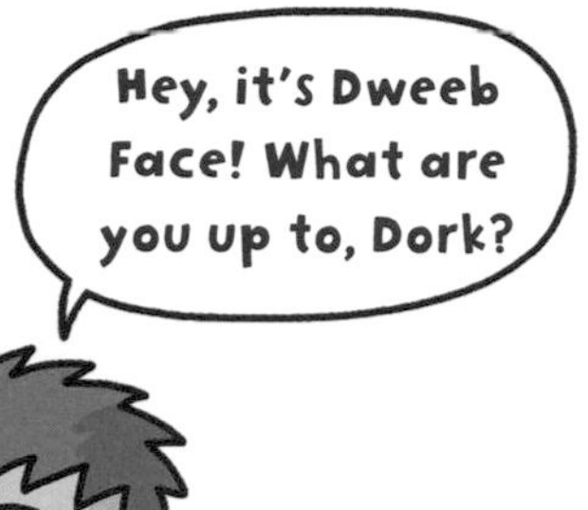
Hey, it's Dweeb Face! What are you up to, Dork?

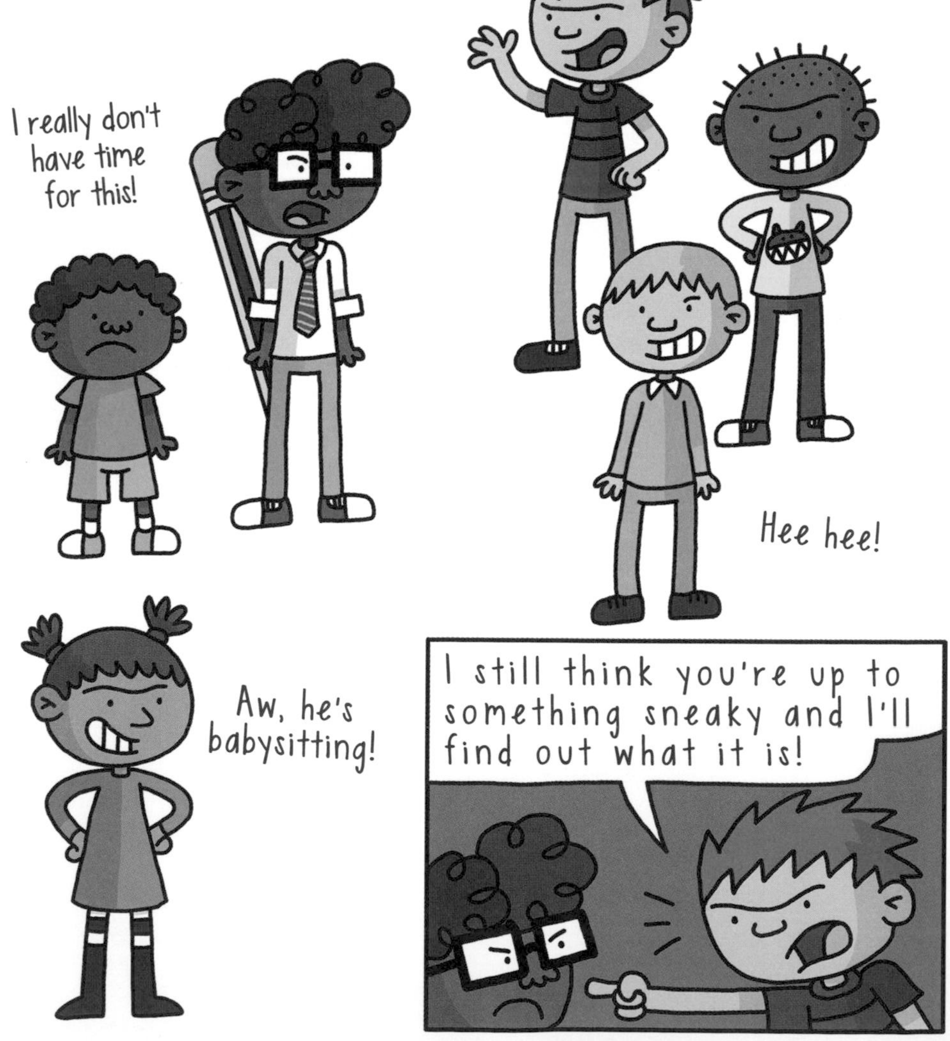
I really don't have time for this!
Hee hee!
Aw, he's babysitting!
I still think you're up to something sneaky and I'll find out what it is!

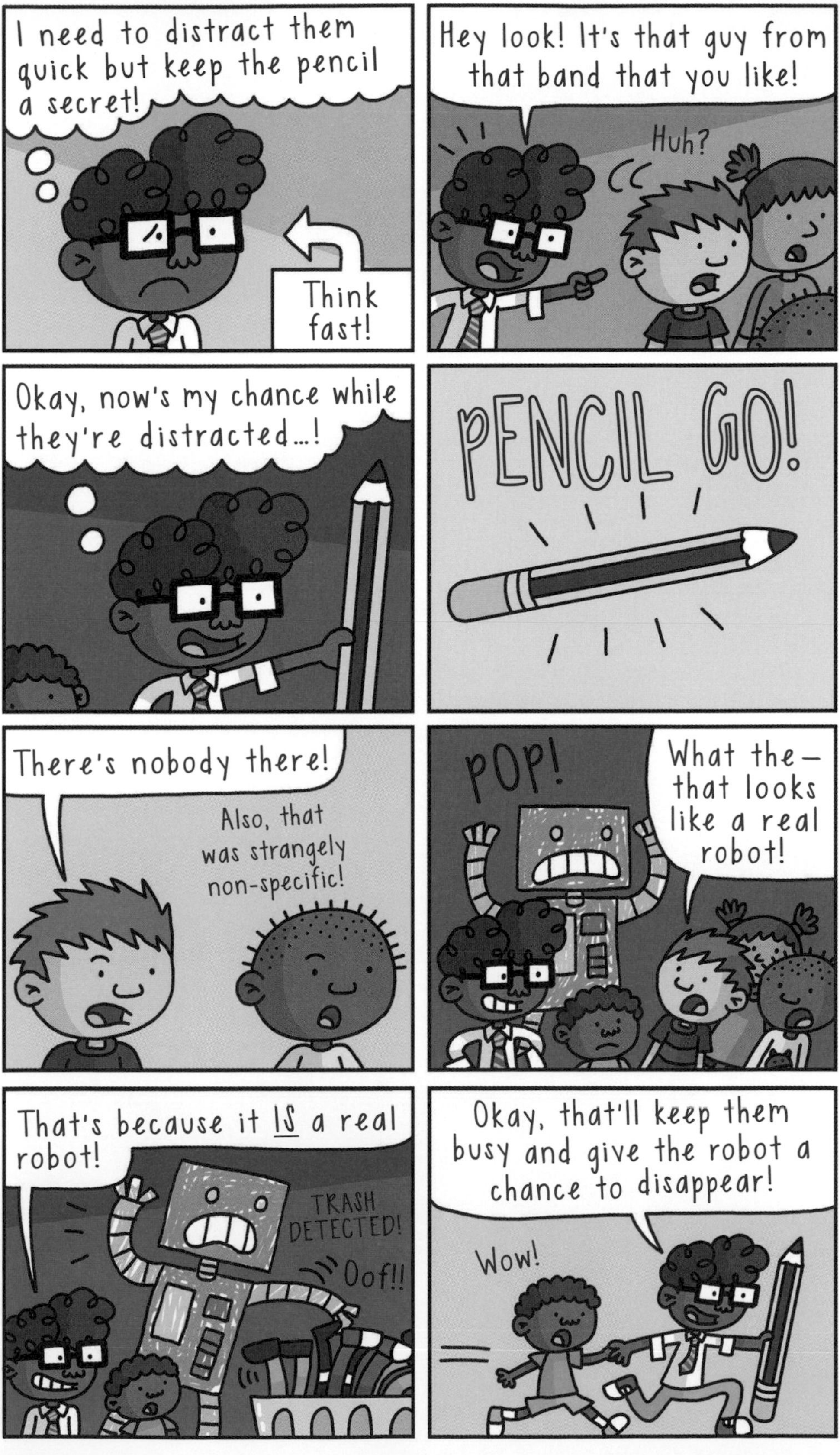
I need to distract them quick but keep the pencil a secret!
Think fast!
Hey look! It's that guy from that band that you like!
Huh?
Okay, now's my chance while they're distracted...!
PENCIL GO!
There's nobody there!
Also, that was strangely non-specific!
POP!
What the— that looks like a real robot!
That's because it IS a real robot!
TRASH DETECTED!
Oof!!
Okay, that'll keep them busy and give the robot a chance to disappear!
Wow!

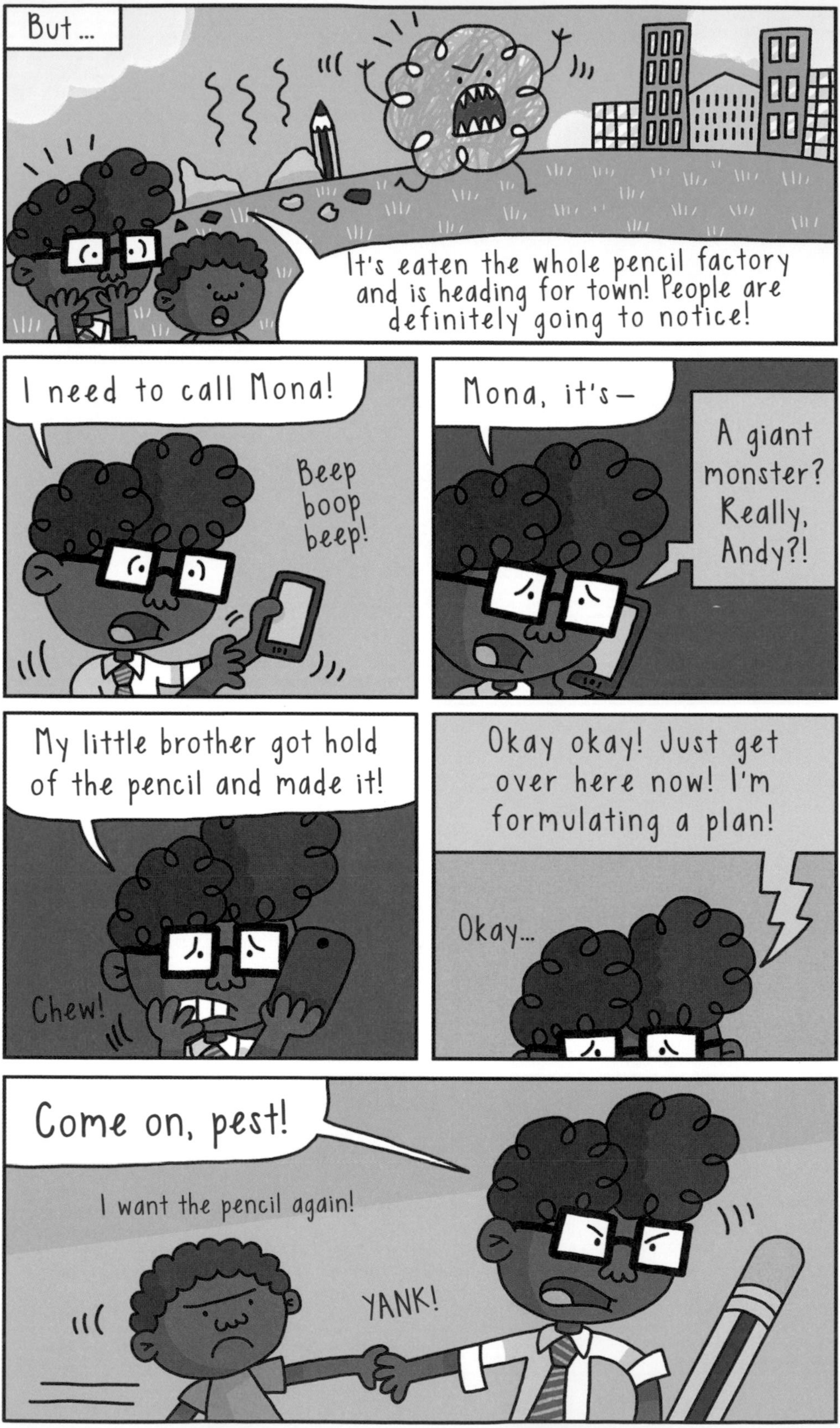
But ...
It's eaten the whole pencil factory and is heading for town! People are definitely going to notice!
I need to call Mona!
Beep boop beep!
Mona, it's—
A giant monster? Really, Andy?!
My little brother got hold of the pencil and made it!
Chew!
Okay okay! Just get over here now! I'm formulating a plan!
Okay...
Come on, pest!
I want the pencil again!
YANK!

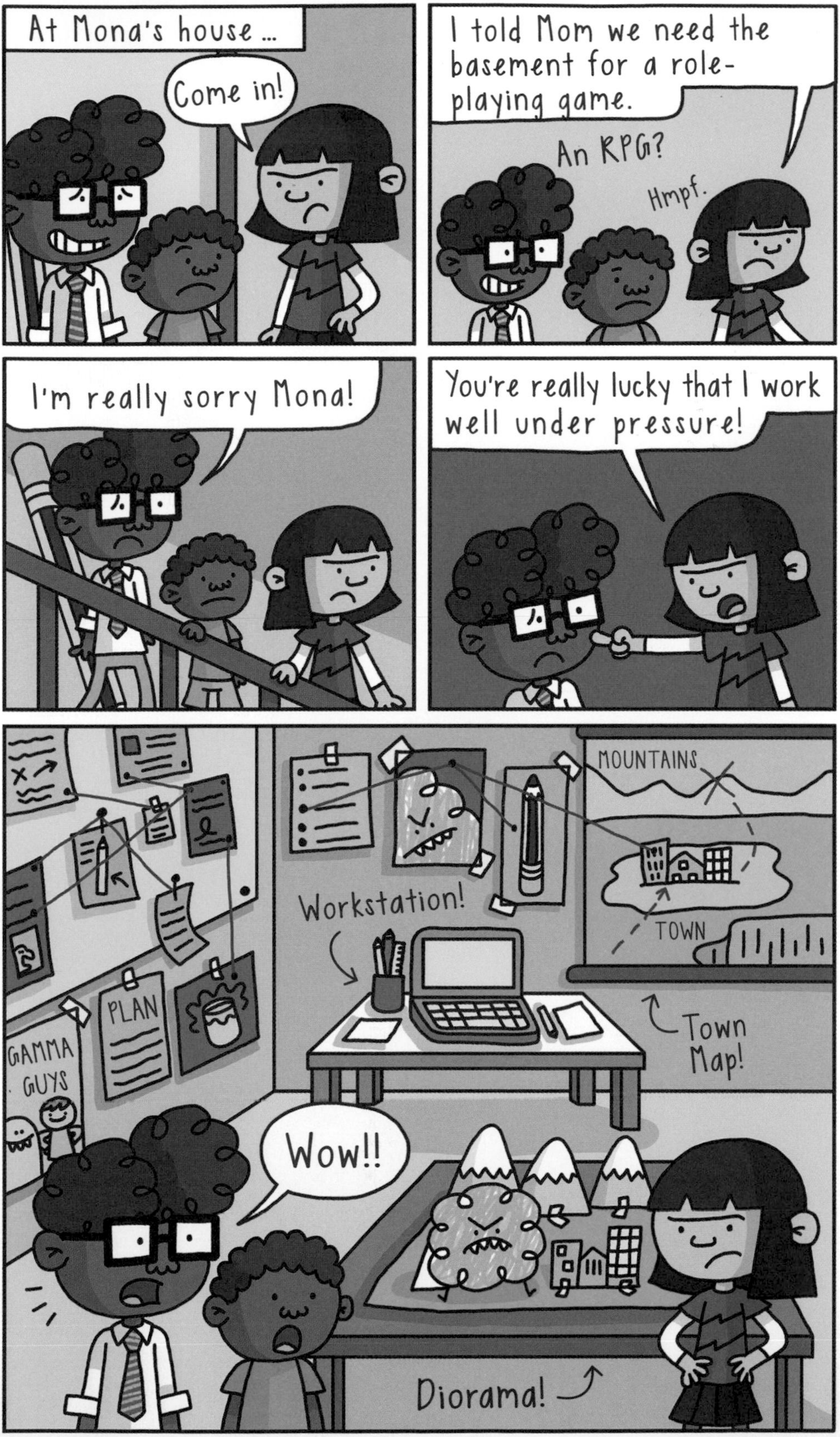
At Mona's house ...
Come in!
I told Mom we need the basement for a role-playing game.
An RPG?
Hmpf.
I'm really sorry Mona!
You're really lucky that I work well under pressure!
MOUNTAINS
TOWN
Workstation!
Town Map!
PLAN
GAMMA GUYS
Wow!!
Diorama!

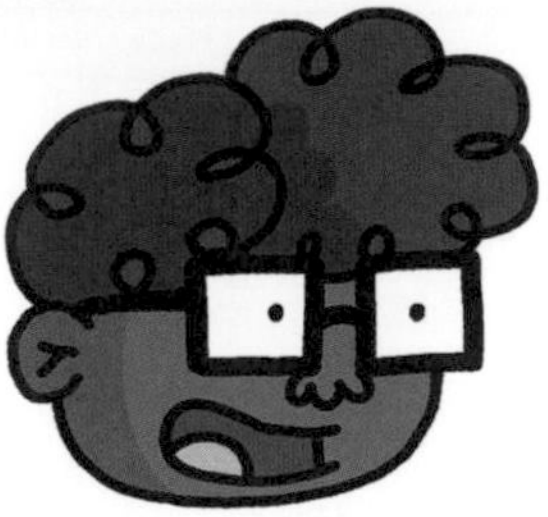

"This is <u>AMAZING!</u> How did you have time to do all of this?"

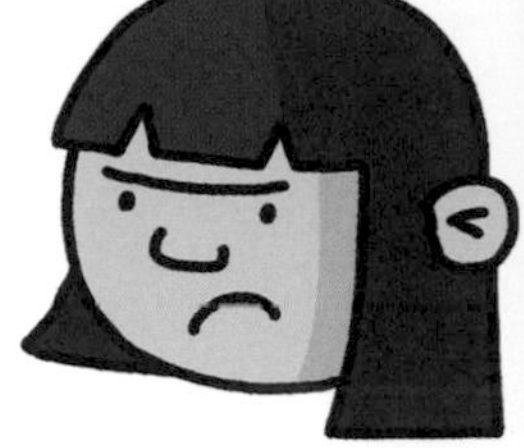

"It's not that different from planning a campaign for 'Crypts & Critters.' But never mind that ..."

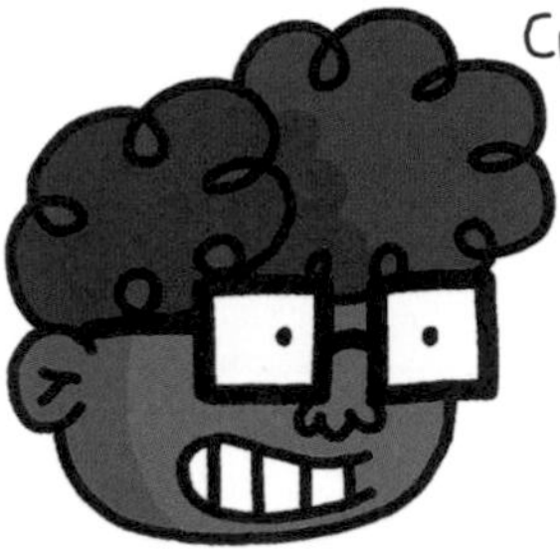

"It's like a proper operations room! You are the COOLEST DWEEB ever!"

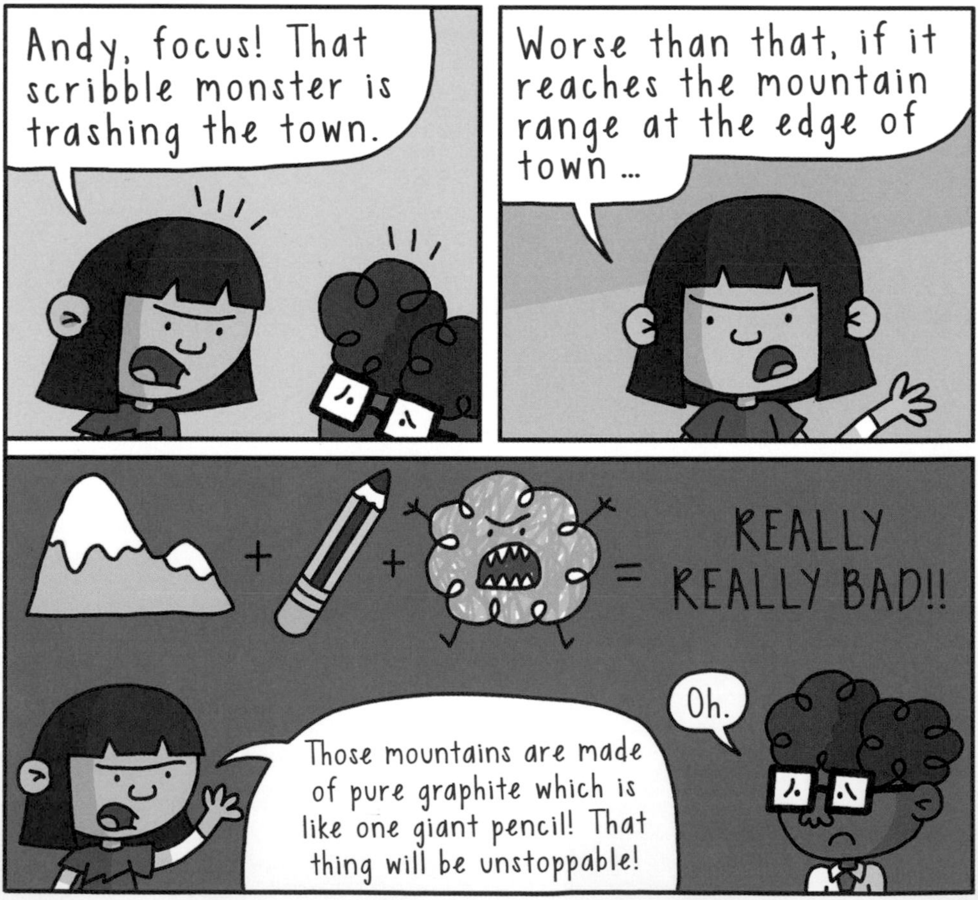

Andy, focus! That scribble monster is trashing the town.
Worse than that, if it reaches the mountain range at the edge of town ...
+ + = REALLY REALLY BAD!!
Those mountains are made of pure graphite which is like one giant pencil! That thing will be unstoppable!
Oh.

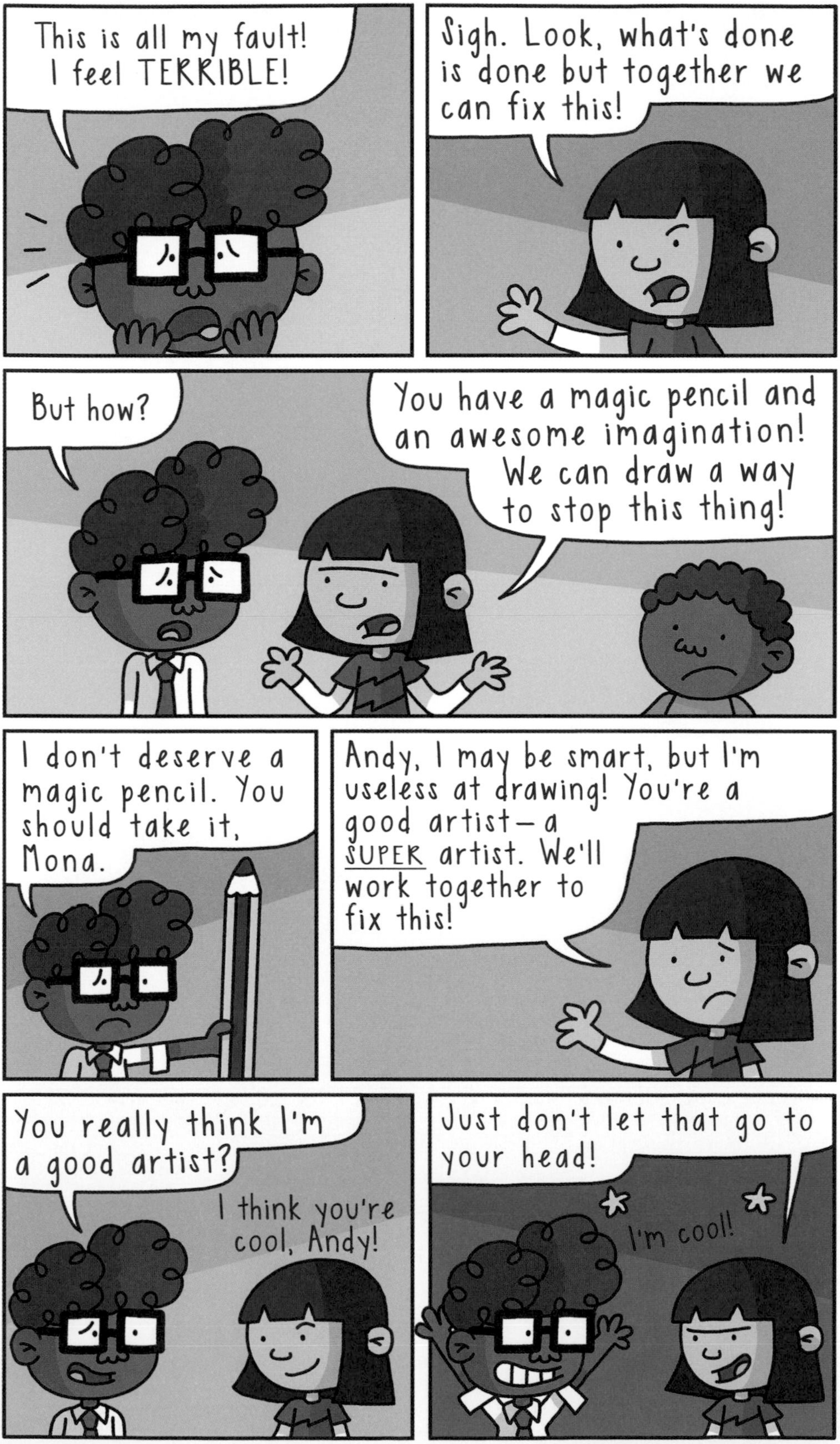
This is all my fault! I feel TERRIBLE!
Sigh. Look, what's done is done but together we can fix this!
But how?
You have a magic pencil and an awesome imagination! We can draw a way to stop this thing!
I don't deserve a magic pencil. You should take it, Mona.
Andy, I may be smart, but I'm useless at drawing! You're a good artist—a SUPER artist. We'll work together to fix this!
You really think I'm a good artist?
I think you're cool, Andy!
Just don't let that go to your head!
I'm cool!

"NOW," said Mona, all business again, "I took the liberty of designing you a costume.

Nobody can know you have a magic pencil.

Or, you know, realize that we're the cause of all this trouble."

"Gasp! Like a **REAL SUPERHERO!**"

"Here, SUPER DWEEB!

Go and get changed!"

said Mona.

"Super Dweeb?" I grumbled.

"Can't I have a cooler name?"

"Nope. I made the **COSTUME**, so I get to choose the name!"

"Hmph. Fair enough!"

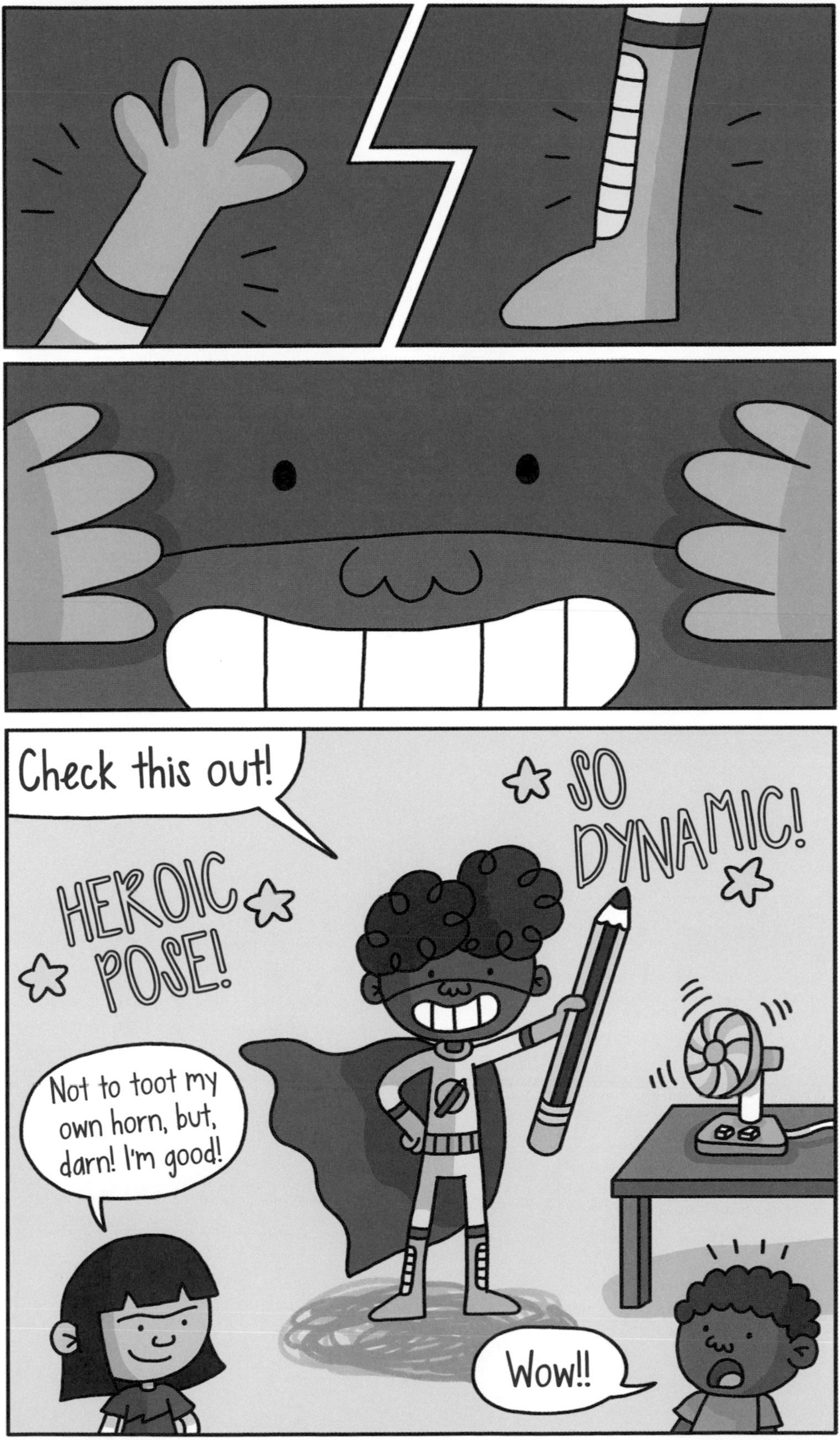
Check this out!
HEROIC POSE!
SO DYNAMIC!
Not to toot my own horn, but, darn! I'm good!
Wow!!

"Okay, no more heroic posing" said Mona. "We need to stop that monster!"

"But... how? It's <u>*HUGE!*</u>" I said.

Mona handed me an earpiece. "Here, put this in your ear. I'll be right here to guide you and try to figure out how we can defeat that thing!"

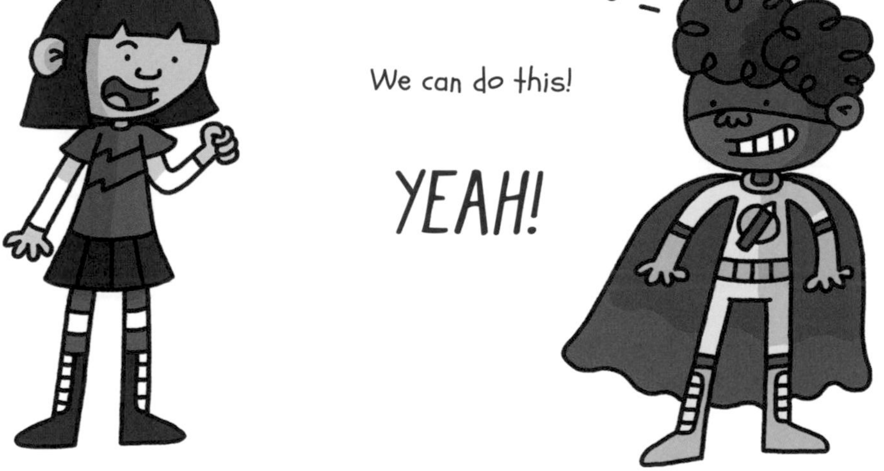
We can do this!
YEAH!

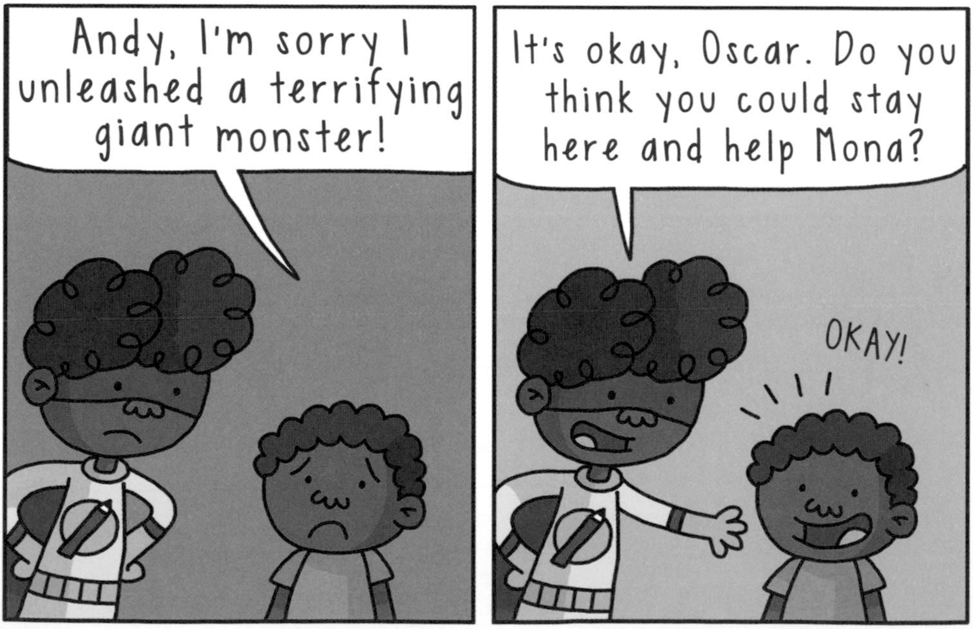
Andy, I'm sorry I unleashed a terrifying giant monster!
It's okay, Oscar. Do you think you could stay here and help Mona?
OKAY!

Chapter 6 The Awesome Battle

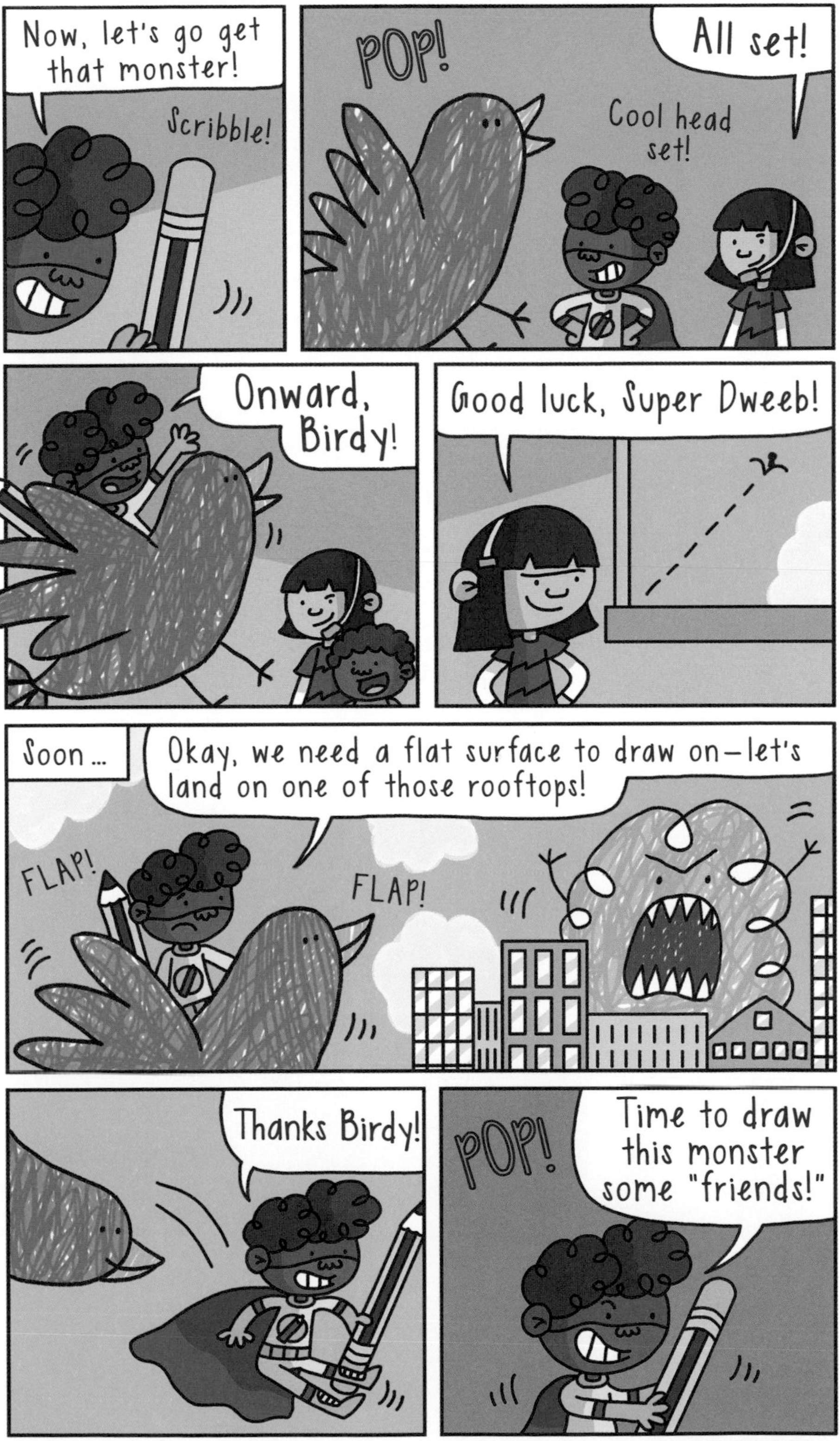
Now, let's go get that monster!
Scribble!
POP!
All set!
Cool head set!
Onward, Birdy!
Good luck, Super Dweeb!
Soon...
Okay, we need a flat surface to draw on—let's land on one of those rooftops!
FLAP!
FLAP!
Thanks Birdy!
POP!
Time to draw this monster some "friends!"

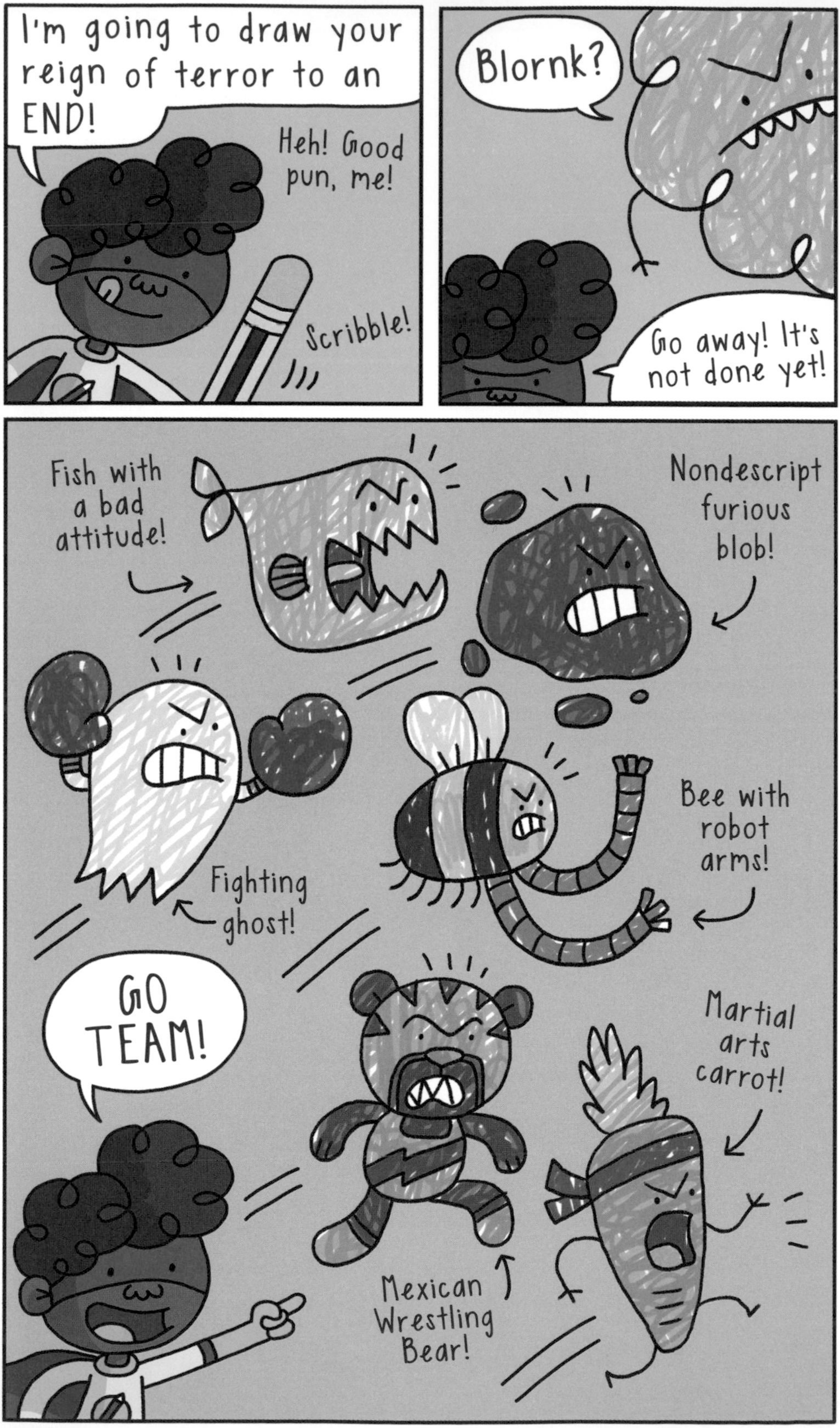

I'm going to draw your reign of terror to an END!
Heh! Good pun, me!
Scribble!
Blornk?
Go away! It's not done yet!
Fish with a bad attitude!
Nondescript furious blob!
Fighting ghost!
Bee with robot arms!
GO TEAM!
Martial arts carrot!
Mexican Wrestling Bear!

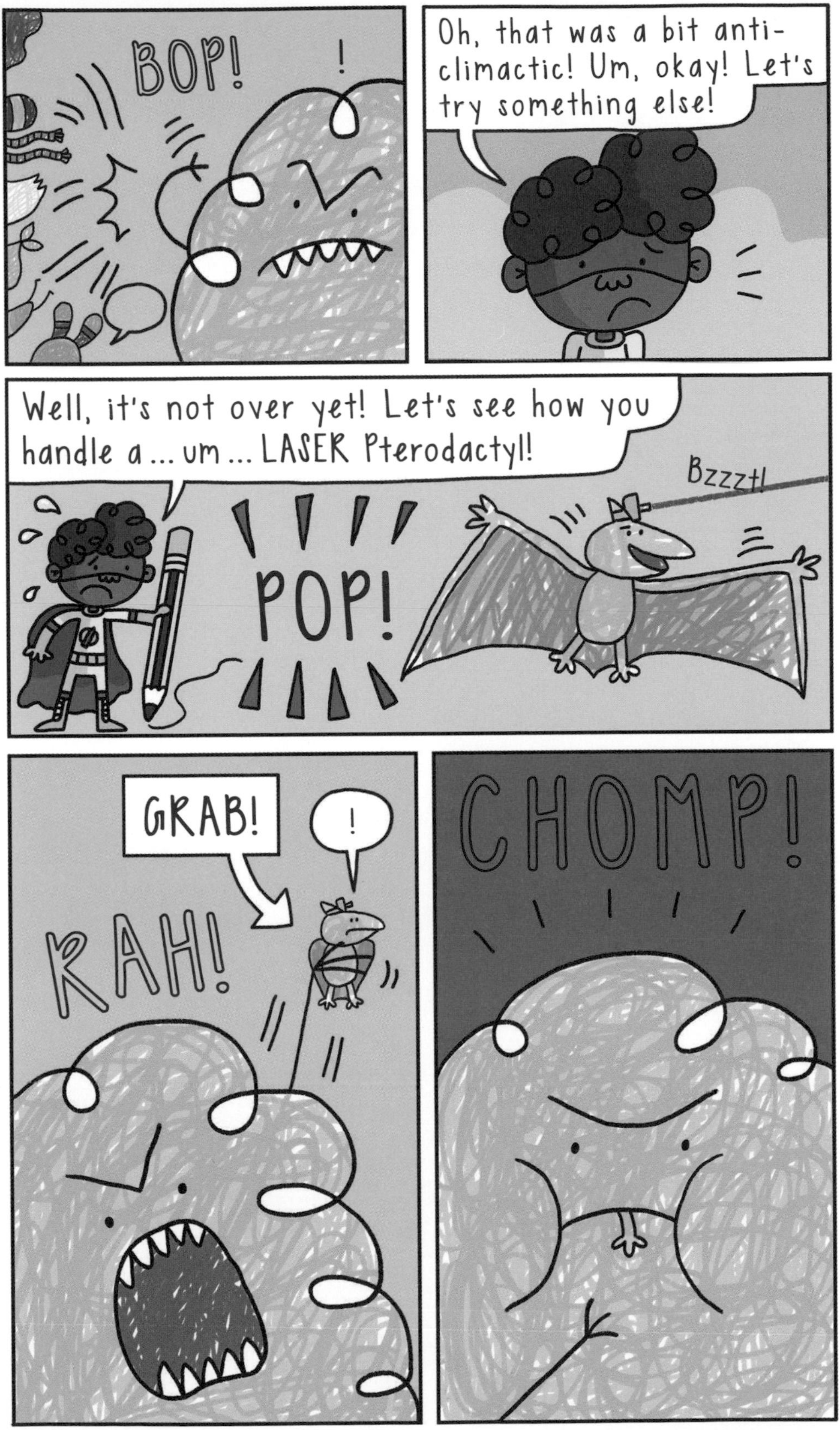
BOP!
!
Oh, that was a bit anti-climactic! Um, okay! Let's try something else!
Well, it's not over yet! Let's see how you handle a ... um ... LASER Pterodactyl!
POP!
Bzzzt!
GRAB!
!
RAH!
CHOMP!

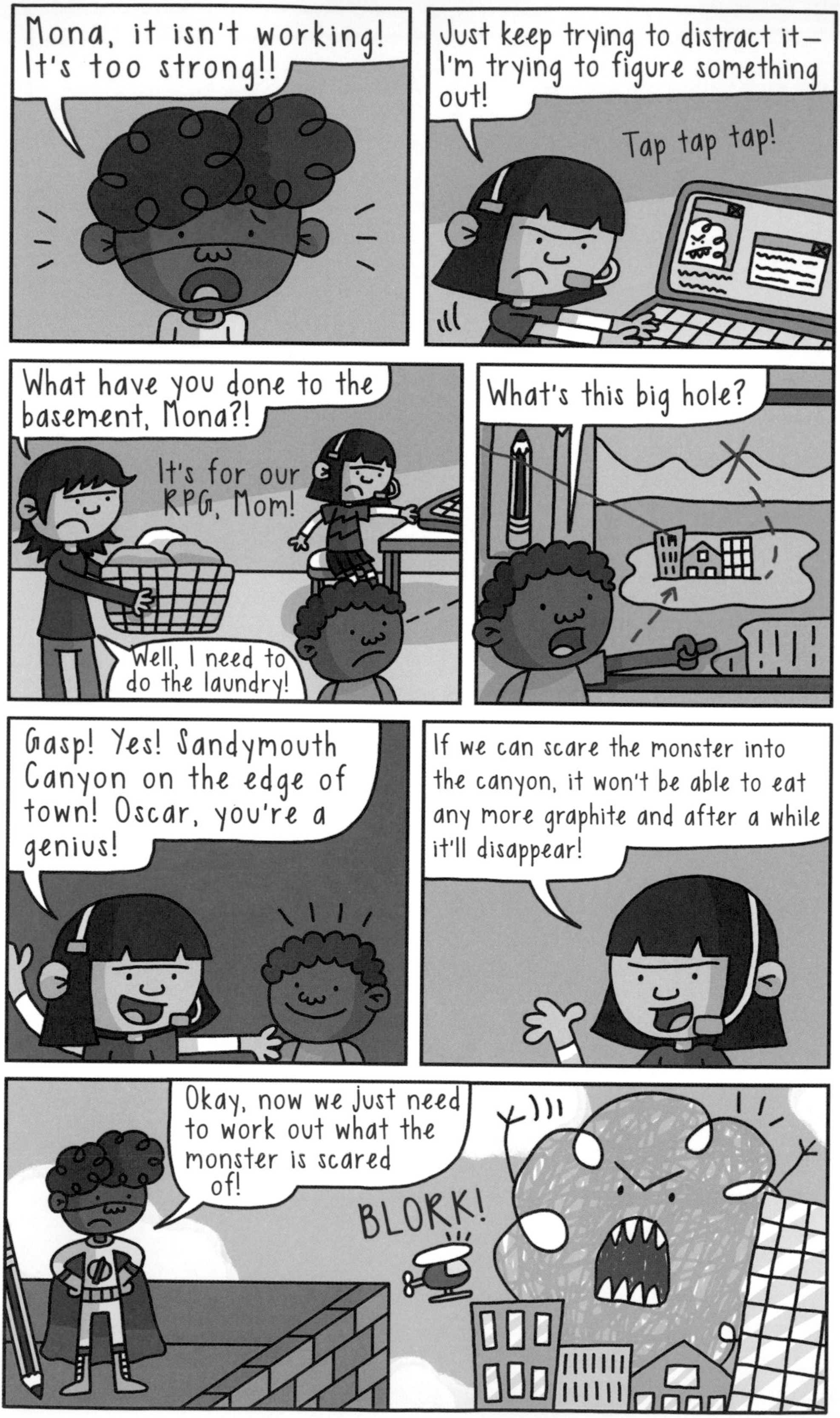
Mona, it isn't working! It's too strong!!
Just keep trying to distract it— I'm trying to figure something out!
Tap tap tap!
What have you done to the basement, Mona?!
It's for our RPG, Mom!
Well, I need to do the laundry!
What's this big hole?
Gasp! Yes! Sandymouth Canyon on the edge of town! Oscar, you're a genius!
If we can scare the monster into the canyon, it won't be able to eat any more graphite and after a while it'll disappear!
Okay, now we just need to work out what the monster is scared of!
BLORK!

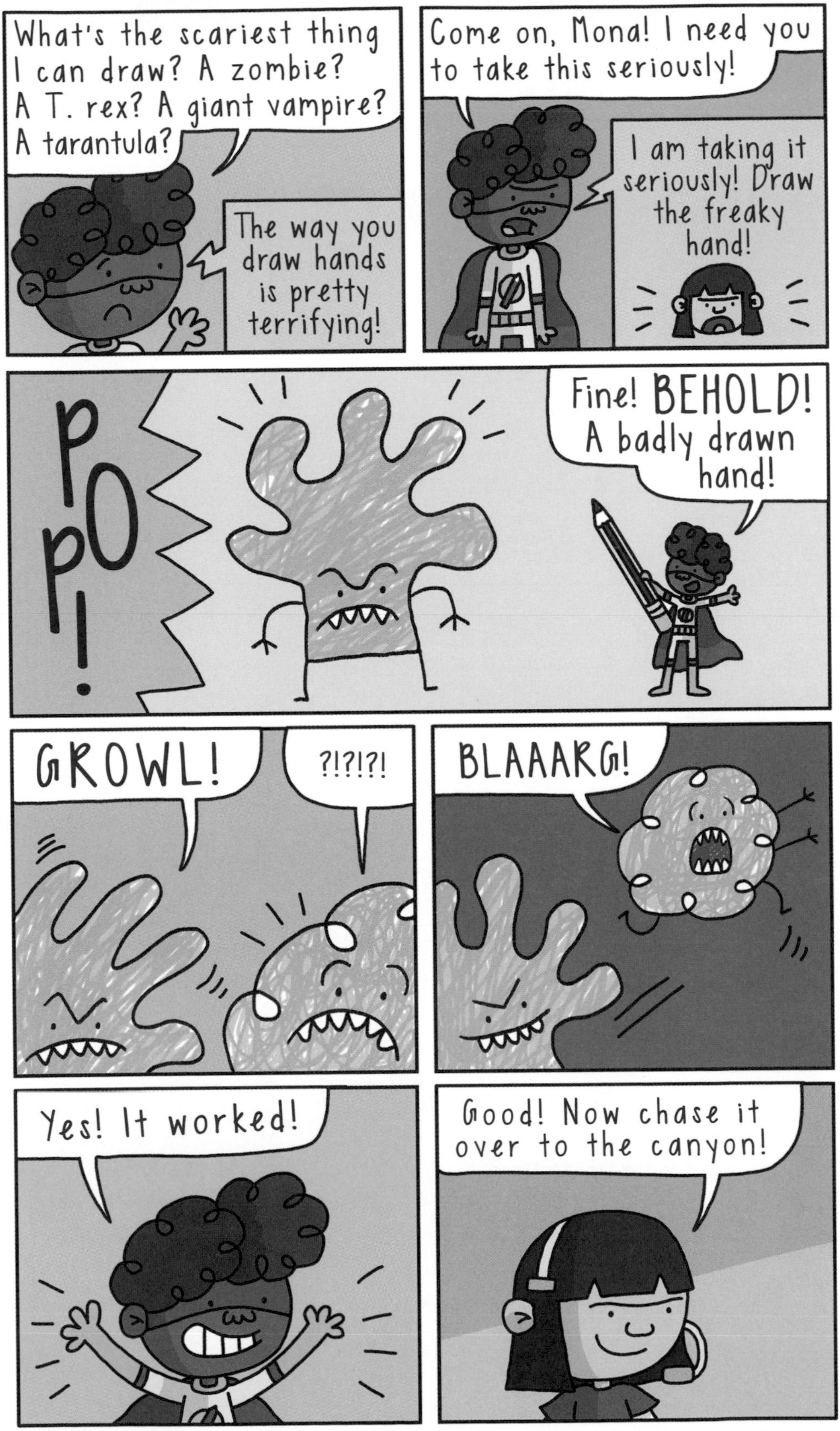
What's the scariest thing I can draw? A zombie? A T. rex? A giant vampire? A tarantula?
The way you draw hands is pretty terrifying!
Come on, Mona! I need you to take this seriously!
I am taking it seriously! Draw the freaky hand!
POP!
Fine! BEHOLD! A badly drawn hand!
GROWL!
?!?!?!
BLAAARG!
Yes! It worked!
Good! Now chase it over to the canyon!

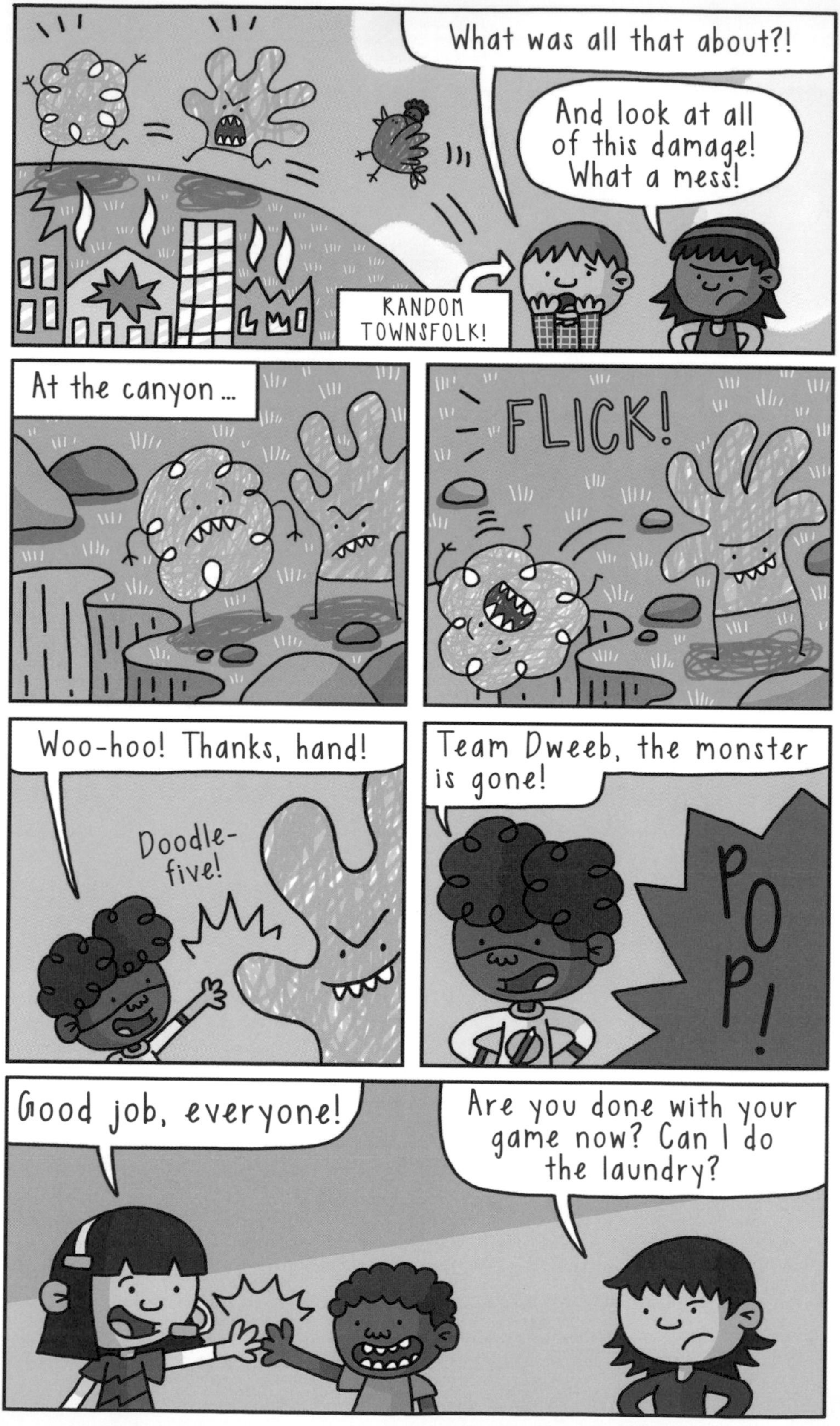
What was all that about?!
And look at all of this damage! What a mess!
RANDOM TOWNSFOLK!
At the canyon ...
FLICK!
Woo-hoo! Thanks, hand!
Doodle-five!
Team Dweeb, the monster is gone!
POP!
Good job, everyone!
Are you done with your game now? Can I do the laundry?

Back at Dweeb HQ ...

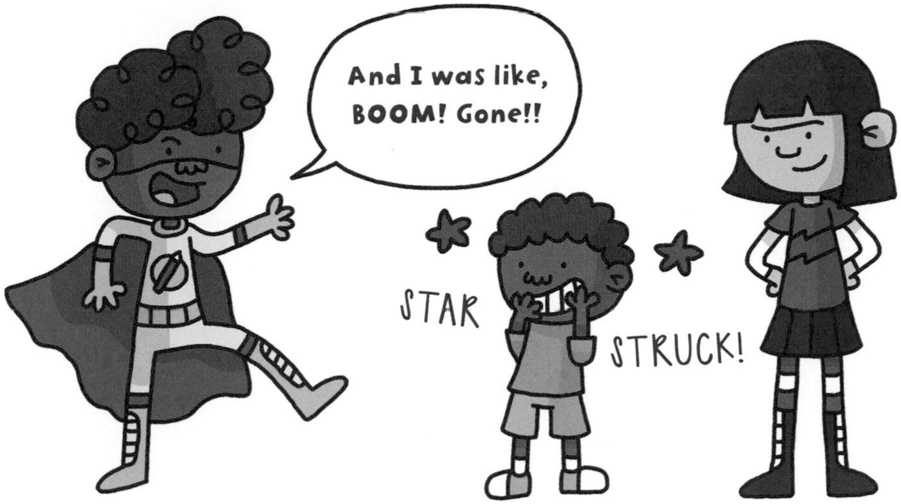
And I was like, BOOM! Gone!!
STAR
STRUCK!

"Okay," said Mona, "now let's have a chat about

RESPONSIBILITY! "

"Heh heh!" I laughed. "Believe me, I think we've both learned our lesson!"

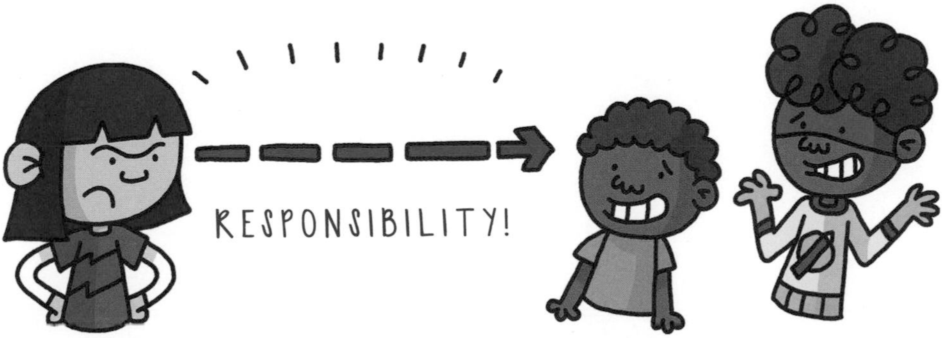
RESPONSIBILITY!

"Fine," sighed Mona. "Well, HOPEFULLY we won't have any more pencil-based excitement for a while. And if anyone asks where we've been today, just give them a MYSTERIOUS LOOK.

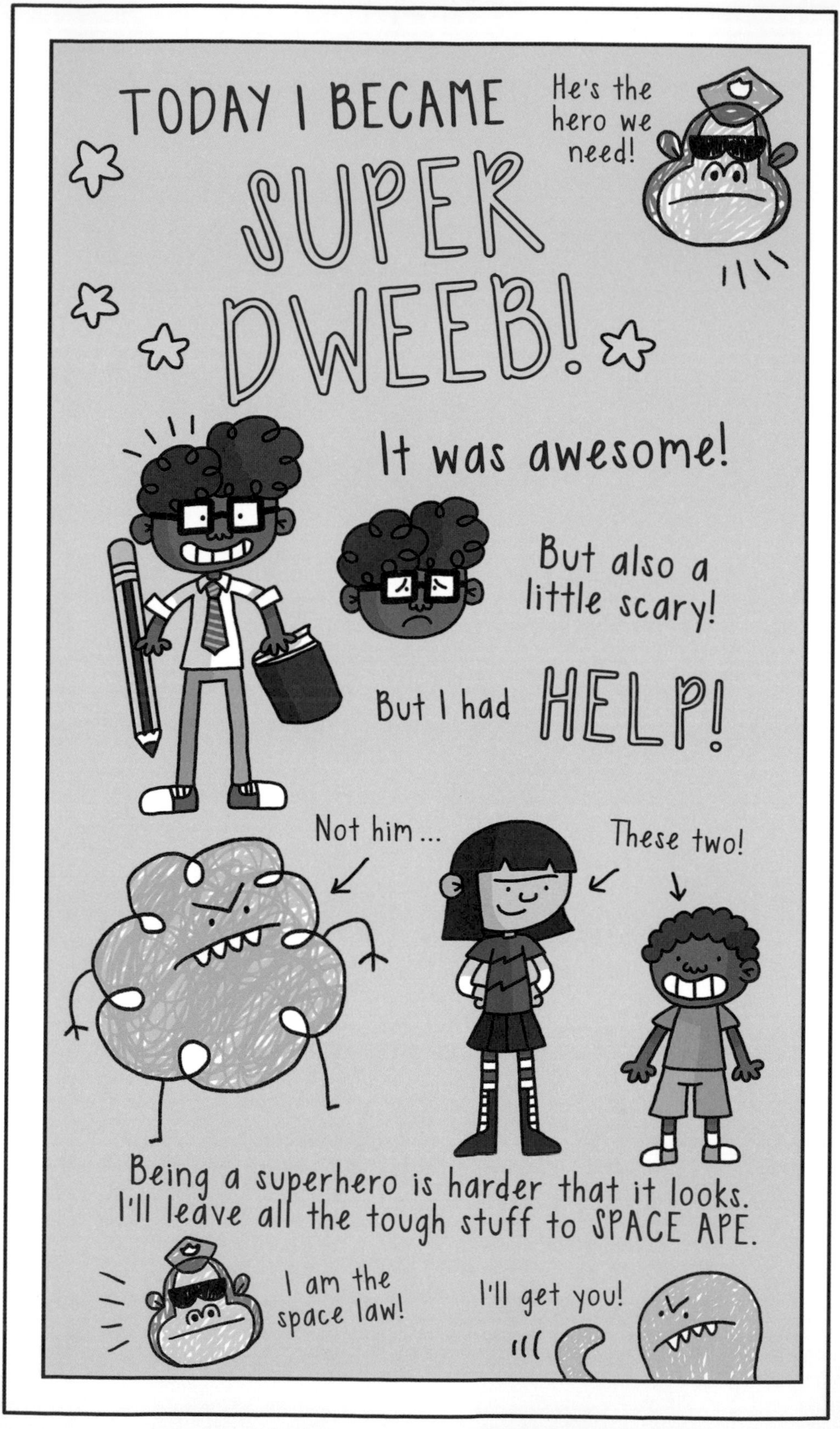
TODAY I BECAME
SUPER DWEEB!
He's the hero we need!
It was awesome!
But also a little scary!
But I had HELP!
Not him ...
These two!
Being a superhero is harder that it looks. I'll leave all the tough stuff to SPACE APE.
I am the space law!
I'll get you!

Oscar came to see me in my room.

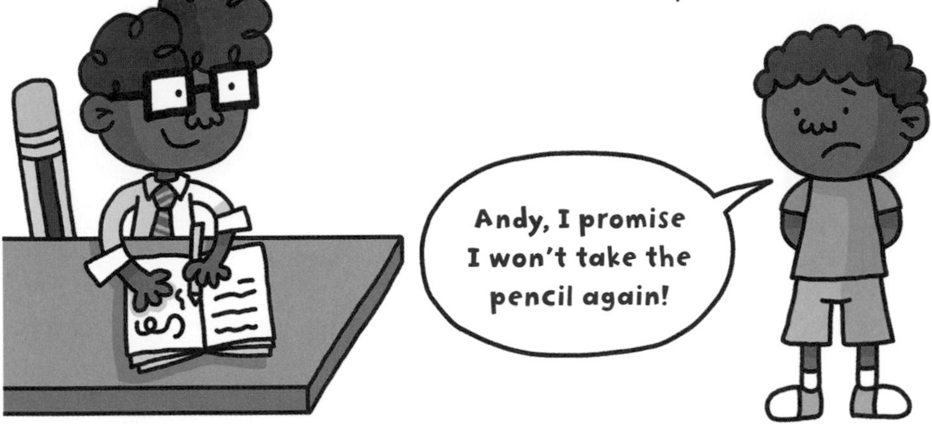
Andy, I promise I won't take the pencil again!

"You know, I MIGHT need some help from time to time, not just with the pencil. You saved the day with your canyon idea," I said.

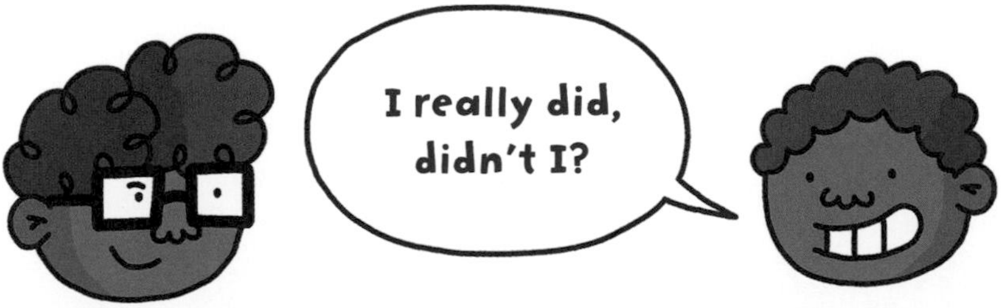
I really did, didn't I?

"Just don't let it go to your head, okay?"

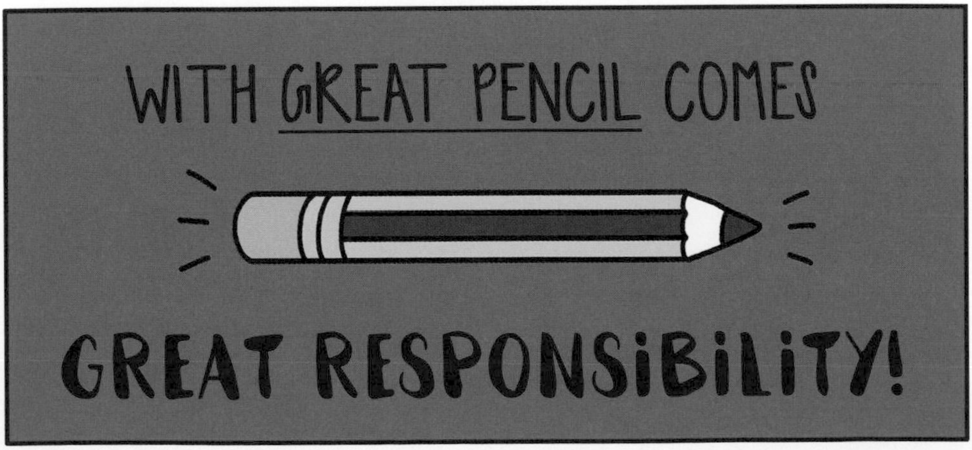
WITH GREAT PENCIL COMES
GREAT RESPONSIBILITY!

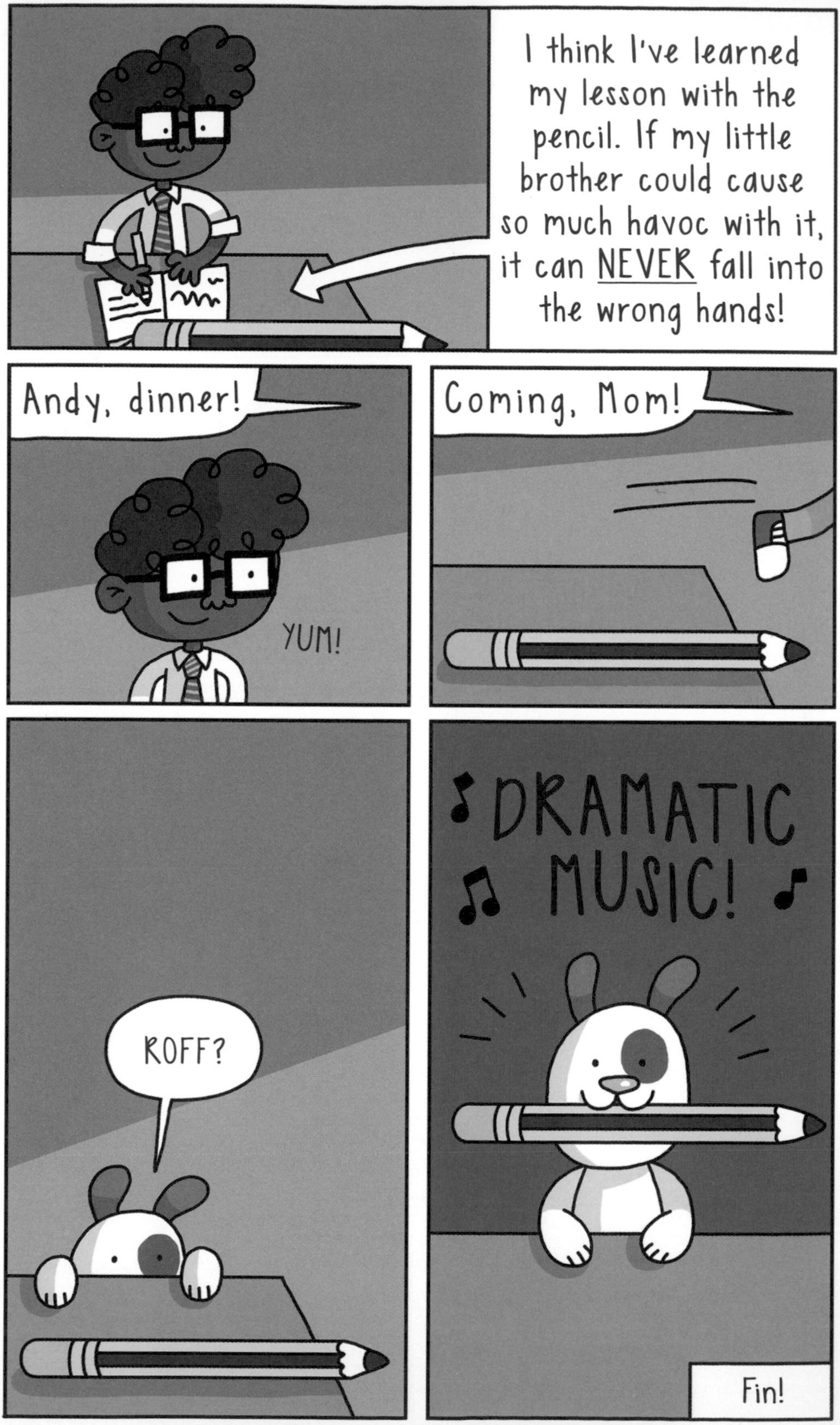
I think I've learned my lesson with the pencil. If my little brother could cause so much havoc with it, it can NEVER fall into the wrong hands!
Andy, dinner!
YUM!
Coming, Mom!
ROFF?
DRAMATIC MUSIC!
Fin!